REICHE, Dietlof

Freddy in peril

Also available in *The Golden Hamster Saga*. . .

FREDDY ON THE LOOSE
FREDDY TO THE RESCUE

CHAPTER ONE

IT ALL STARTED THAT NIGHT.

It had started before that, of course, but that was the night I realized whose life was at stake: mine. Professor Fleischkopf was after me – he aimed to get me in his clutches.

i was in mortal danger.

It must have been around midnight. Enrico and Caruso, the singing guinea pigs, had finally shut up, and Sir William, the civilized tomcat, had retired to his blanket. Mr John wasn't there. He'd had to go away for a few days.

I was seated at the keyboard of the Mac, working on a short story. Nights are my favourite time for writing. For one thing, because we golden hamsters are always wide awake at that hour (science teachers describe us as "nocturnally active"), and, for another, because it's when I have the Mac all to myself (Mr John normally uses it for his translations during the day). What I was writing that

night is beside the point (OK, it was a horror story titled "The Curse of the Weasel"). In any event, my paws were typing away briskly.

I worked away in silence.

Of course, there were all kinds of noises to be heard. The ticking of Mr John's alarm clock, for instance, and the purring of the fridge in the kitchen, the dull roar of the traffic on the street below, and the hum of the Mac and the click of the keys as I pressed them down with my paws. But none of these noises sounded particularly loud, even to a hamster's highly sensitive ears, and besides, they were normal at that time of night.

I continued working in silence.

And then, just as I was rereading what I'd typed on the

screen, I heard the front door open downstairs. This wasn't unusual in itself. We live in a big apartment building (on the very top floor), and people sometimes come home late. Besides, the door to the street is never locked. In a moment I was sure I would hear it shut, followed by footsteps on the stairs and the sound of a neighbour's door being opened.

But no, this time it was nothing like that.

The front door must have been closed so carefully, not even I had heard it. I strained my ears. Then came the sound of very soft footsteps. Someone was tiptoeing up the stairs.

The footsteps drew nearer. They didn't come to a halt outside any of the apartments below us, but continued to climb, growing louder and louder.

They reached the top of the stairs.

I stiffened.

Silence.

There was a sudden, faint jingling sound, as if someone had removed a bunch of keys from his pocket.

Another silence.

Then two things happened: first, I heard someone insert something in the lock; second, a smell hit me.

A sudden, acrid stench of sulphur.

I realized who was standing outside the door.

It was yesterday's visitor – the man who had suddenly appeared in Mr John's study.

It was Professor Fleischkopf.

I hadn't smelled him at first. He was tall and thin, with gleaming, rimless glasses, and he stank of some sulphurous antidandruff shampoo.

"Good morning," he said. He spoke with a strange, guttural accent I'd never heard before. "Permit me to introduce myself. I'm Professor Schmidt."

I didn't know he was lying, not at that point, but I suspected it. Why? Because he'd hesitated for a moment before saying "Schmidt".

"Huh?" said Mr John, getting up. He'd been sitting in front of the Mac, working on a translation that had to be finished before he went away. "What can I do for you?" he

4

asked – very politely, although it must have miffed him that this Professor Schmidt had breezed straight into the apartment after a cursory knock. Mr John doesn't always lock the door when he's home, but he always keeps his cool. Well, nearly always.

"I'm eager to improve my English," said Professor Fleischkopf, alias Professor Schmidt, "and I'm told you give language lessons. German lessons to Americans, English lessons to Germans, correct?" The Adam's apple in his scrawny neck bobbed up and down as he spoke. I could see this very clearly because he was standing quite close to my cage. (Unlike all its other senses, a hamster's eyesight is nothing to write home about.)

"Yes, I do give lessons," said Mr John, "but I can't take on any more students right now."

"Oh, really? Too bad." Professor Schmidt was trying to sound regretful, I guess, but for some reason he didn't seem to mind that his lesson idea wasn't going to work. "In that case, there's nothing to be done." He looked around the room – and then he saw me. Or rather, he *stared* at me. My cage is kept on a bookshelf at eye level, and since I was standing on my hind legs, clinging to the little door, Professor Fleischkopf and I were face to face.

I'D NEVER LOOKED INTO A COLDER, MORE SINISTER PAIR OF EYES.

The Professor stared at me with a totally expressionless face. He froze me, as it were, with his ice-cold gaze, and I bared my teeth in an involuntary snarl. Time stood still, or so it seemed, because the whole incident must have been over within seconds. Suddenly, without a word, he turned away and walked to the door.

"Have a nice day," he said and departed as abruptly as he had come.

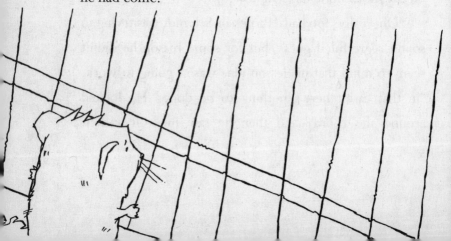

The throat-catching, sulphurous smell lingered in the room for a long time after he'd left.

Now, in the middle of the night, I detected that smell again. It was seeping into the apartment through the cracks around the front door. Professor Fleischkopf had to be standing just outside.

What was more, he'd inserted something in the lock. **He was trying to break in!**

I rose on my hind legs, fur bristling.

I was paralysed at first, but then I pulled myself together. Darting to the opposite end of the desk, I climbed down my miniature rope ladder at top speed, reached the floor, and scurried into the room next door, where Sir William was lying on his cat blanket. He was fast asleep.

"Sir William!" I hissed.

No reaction.

"Sir William!"

A subdued snore, then silence again.

I listened hard. Faint scraping, rattling sounds were coming from the direction of the front door. Professor Fleischkopf was evidently trying to open it with a skeleton key.

"Sir William!"

Still no response.

So I bit him. I bit his paw — not very hard, but it worked. Sir William woke up with a start.

"Freddy!" he said, wringing his paw. "Are you out of your mind? What do you mean by —" He broke off and pricked his ears. "There's someone there. Outside the front door."

"Exactly," I whispered. "He's trying to get in."

We listened. Something was withdrawn from the lock and something else inserted: Professor Fleischkopf was trying another skeleton key.

Sir William sniffed the air. "It's that man from yesterday — the one with the disgusting shampoo. But what's he doing here?"

"He's come to get me."

"You?" Sir William stared down at me, shaking his head. "My dear Freddy, you'll have to explain. Why on earth would anyone —"

Click! went the door.

"He's inside! He's coming!"

"Quick, hide!" hissed Sir William. "Hide somewhere. I'll try to distract him. . . . No, wait!"

"He hasn't broken in after all," I whispered. "Not yet."

"All right, go and look for a hiding place. I'll see what I can do." Sir William sighed. "I wish I could bark. I never thought the day would come when I wished I could—"

"*Ssh!*" I listened. "Footsteps . . . on the stairs . . . going down . . . HE'S RETREATING! He's given up."

"Really?" Sir William listened too. "You're right. Phew!" He lay down on his blanket again, then looked at me.

"Well, I must say! Next time, my young friend, I suggest you administer excitement in slightly smaller doses. But now tell me, why do you think the man was after *you*?"

"It was those eyes of his," I said, and I described how Professor Fleischkopf had focused his ice-cold gaze on me.

"Well, it certainly doesn't sound like love at first sight," said Sir William. "But the question is: why? I mean, what does he want you for?" He thought a moment. "If this Professor Fleischkopf really wants to get you in his clutches, he's bound to try again."

Suddenly Sir William raised his head. "Hey! He introduced himself as Professor Schmidt. How do you know his name is Fleischkopf?"

CHAPTER TWO

BECAUSE, YOUR LORDSHIP, I'm a small but quick-witted rodent who can put two and two together.

I didn't say that to Sir William, of course, not even in fun. He might have misinterpreted it as an affront to his dignity, and he can turn very nasty on such occasions.

So I said modestly, "Remember the other visitor we had yesterday?"

"Of course I do. That woman. That, that. . ."

"Linda Carson," I said helpfully.

"Right. But. . ." Sir William shook his head as if trying to rearrange his thoughts. "What has Linda Carson got to do with Professor Fleischkopf?"

Nothing, to begin with.

Yesterday the telephone rang: that was all that happened at first.

"Hello?" Mr John said. "Yes, that's right, speaking. . .

Oh, I see, a journalist. . . And you're doing an article on translators? Sure, why not? However, Miss, er, Carson, I'm afraid I'll have to take a rain check. I'm going away. . . Yes, I'm sorry, this evening . . . for a few days. . . Oh, I see. . . But I haven't packed yet. . . All right, then. Yes, I know the bar, it's just around the corner from here. . . In an hour's time? OK, see you then."

Mr John replaced the receiver and turned to me. I'd been sitting beside the keyboard watching him at work (one never stops learning). He rubbed his nose thoughtfully (he's got a sizable nose and a sizable pair of bushy eyebrows) and said, "Well, kid, I'm still not sure I ought to leave you animals on your own for several days." He sighed. "Anything might happen."

Nothing will happen, Mr John. You're going away, but you'll be back in a few days.

I had typed those words on the keyboard so they appeared on the screen. The trouble is, we animals can understand humans, but humans can't understand us. With Sir William and Enrico and Caruso, I talk in

12

Interanimal. That's a kind of telepathic language all mammals can speak – all except for humans, of course. (Why I whispered telepathically when Professor Fleischkopf was trying to break in, I frankly don't know. Probably for dramatic effect.)

Anyway, I typed, *Sophie will look after us.* My former mistress had promised to come and feed us every day after school.

Mr John heaved another sigh. Then he nodded, pulled up his chair, deleted the words I'd written on the screen, and went on with his translation.

The second interruption of the afternoon was a knock at the front door. Mr John growled something unintelligible and walked to the door.

I heard him open it and expected him to say, "Yes? What do you want?" in an irritable voice, but he didn't. All he said was, "Oh!"

Almost at the same moment, the study was invaded by a scent of apple and peach blossom, which – I can't put it any other way – simply sent me into raptures.

"Hello," I heard. "We spoke on the phone a little earlier." It was a woman's voice – not one of those high-pitched, squeaky voices that a hamster's ears find so painful, but soft and melodious. "I managed to get away sooner than expected, so I thought to myself: why wait in the bar on my own?"

Mr John cleared his throat. "Er, yes, why indeed?" A pause, then, "Won't you, er, come in?"

"What a relief," she said. "I was beginning to think I'd have to wait outside."

Linda Carson, who had lustrous red hair, was nearly as tall as Mr John. She looked around the room. "This must be your study," she said. "Forgive me, I don't mean to be nosy, but it's part of a journalist's job." She laughed. "Or did I become a journalist because I'm nosy by nature?"

14

Mr John smiled. "Ask me any questions you like."

At that moment, Sir William came stalking into the room.

"Why, he's huge!" Linda Carson exclaimed. "Jet-black all over too. A tom?"

Mr John nodded. "His name is William."

"And the guinea pigs?" She had spotted the cage through the door to the next room. "What cute little fellows!"

"Those are Enrico and Caruso," Mr John told her. "And that guy there" – he pointed to the desk – "is Freddy."

Because I was partly obscured by the keyboard (which was probably why Linda Carson had failed to notice me), I scampered to the middle of the desk, sat up, and begged. Then – one likes to show oneself at one's best, after all – I waved to her. I mean I actually waved: I raised my right forepaw above my head, as high as I could, and waved it to and fro. I still believe I'm the only golden hamster in the world capable of doing such a thing. Linda Carson uttered a cry of delight. "He's waving! He's waving to me! That's incredible!"

She came over to the desk. "And he's looking at me like he understands every word."

YOU SAID IT, LADY.

Mr John, standing just behind her, gave me a little shake of the head.

Don't worry, Mr John, I won't give myself away. The fact that I can read and write will remain top secret, just like I promised you.

Linda Carson had bent over me. "Hello there, Freddy," she said, enveloping me in her apple-and-peach-blossom scent. "Delighted to make your acquaintance."

Likewise, lady.

She straightened up. "Aren't they wonderful, living creatures like these?" she said. "We call them animals, but they're inhabitants of this planet just like us. We've no right to torture them." She turned to Mr John. "Sorry. Cruelty to animals is an obsession of mine. I don't mean to bore you with it."

"No need to apologize," said Mr John.

"I'd like to explain, though." Linda Carson indicated his chair. "May I?"

Mr John nodded, and she sat down.

"A few weeks ago I wrote an article about animal experiments. To be more specific, it was about some golden hamsters that had been subjected to frightful experiments. Purely scientific experiments, of course, and purely for the benefit of humanity, so scientists always claim."

"Sure," said Mr John, "like those animal experiments on behalf of the cosmetics industry."

Linda Carson nodded. "But in this case something different was involved. I was on the track of a scientist who carries out research into the intelligence of rodents. For

this he takes the brains of live golden hamsters apart —
literally. I wanted to put a stop to his activities."

"And?" said Mr John.

"There's a rule in journalism: never let your pen run
away with you. I disregarded that rule, unfortunately.
I was so mad at the scientist in question, I referred to
him in my article as a butcher." She fell silent. "I had to
apologize to the man, and my boss really chewed me out.
Our newspaper was compelled to print a reply."

"A reply?"

"Yes, the man was allowed to publish an article
explaining why he *isn't* a butcher. It isn't actually illegal,
what he does."

"Is that a fact?" Mr John shook his head. "And what's
his name?"

"Fleischkopf," said Linda Carson. "Professor Fleischkopf."

CHAPTER THREE

SIR WILLIAM HAD JUMPED to his feet. "You mean," he said, his green eyes glowing, "that Professor Fleischkopf is after you because he wants to examine your brain?"

"Dissect, not examine," I said. "He wants to cut it up, and I shall be privileged to watch him at work."

"Stop it. This is no joking matter," Sir William said sternly. He pondered a while. "You can read and write. Is that why he takes such a keen interest in you?"

"Probably," I said and waited for him to ask the inevitable.

I mean, anyone who had heard the story up to this point would be bound to play the detective and say: OK, so those are the facts. The obvious question is. . .

"We must hold a council of war," said Sir William, squaring his shoulders.

Ah well, Sir William is no detective. A wise old

tomcat with a spotless character, yes, but not an astute intellectual capable of asking the right questions.

"We must all put our heads together," he went on.

"All of us?" I asked. "Enrico and Caruso as well?"

"Of course." Sir William looked at me sharply. "They're members of the family, just like you. I wouldn't want to dispense with the advice of two smart cookies like them, not under any circumstances."

Smart cookies? Don't make me laugh. I'd have bet the entire contents of my larder that the two of them hadn't known a thing about Professor Fleischkopf's attempt to break in. Ten to one they'd been fast asleep in their straw like hibernating squirrels.

We went over to the guinea pigs' cage.

Enrico and Caruso were sitting bolt upright in the entrance, wide awake, their beady little eyes darting this way and that.

They stared at us in silence. Scrawny Enrico has long reddish-white fur and is rather on the small side for

a guinea pig. Caruso is big and plump with a short black-and-white coat.

They waited until we were standing outside their cage.

"Gee, Freddy!" Enrico exclaimed. "What's this you've got yourself mixed up in? It's positively cinematic!"

"Dr Freddy Jekyll and Mr Fleischkopf Hyde!" yelled Caruso.

"Freddy on the Operating Table!" screeched Enrico.

"Professor Fleischkopf Dissects Freddy's Grey Matter!" bellowed Caruso.

They were obviously trying to improve on their own record for tastelessness.

I glanced at Sir William. He was grinning as I expected. At some point in the far distant past, he had decided that Enrico and Caruso were funny, and he stuck to that misconception like glue. To show the guinea pigs what I thought of their witticisms, I twitched the left-hand corner of my upper lip along with the whiskers attached to it.

Their response was swift.

"Oh, look," sighed Enrico, "His Hamstership's expression is accusing. He doesn't find our little jests amusing."

Caruso scratched his head. "What other bright ideas can we suggest? Would logical deductions suit him best?"

"Perhaps," said Enrico, "he wants to plumb the mystery."

"And solve the problem like a private eye," Caruso amplified.

"Well then, my dear Watson," said Enrico, pretending to light a pipe, "let's see what facts we have. What exactly do we know?"

"In the first place," Caruso said eagerly, "a certain Professor Fleischkopf tried to break into this apartment."

"Quite right, Watson. And why? He wanted to steal good old Freddy. We can take that as an established fact."

"Another established fact, Holmes, is that Professor Fleischkopf is interested in good old Freddy for a particular reason. The thing is, Freddy isn't any old golden hamster: Freddy can read and write."

"That, my dear Watson," said Enrico, puffing at his imaginary pipe, "poses a question of some importance." He paused, gazing meditatively into space, then looked up. "How, one can't help wondering, did Professor Fleischkopf *know* that our old pal Freddy can read and write?"

There it was, the question I'd been expecting – and dreading – because the answer to it would not reflect well on me. In fact, it would reflect quite badly.

* * *

It had happened exactly three days ago.

"Freddy?" Mr John called. "Come here, please."

That sounded ominous in itself, like a teacher summoning a student who keeps getting on his nerves. I made my way over to Mr John, who was seated at the Mac. He didn't say, "I want a word with you, kid." He said, "I've got a bone to pick with you, Freddy." I was in for a hard time, that much was obvious, but at that point – forepaw on heart – I didn't have the faintest idea why.

Then Mr John clicked the icon on the screen that accesses the Internet.

I still didn't get it.

Next, Mr John brought up his Web site on the monitor.

And all at once it dawned on me what the trouble was.

I felt tempted to scamper back to the cage and hide myself in my burrow, but a look from Mr John rooted me to the spot. I was forced to survey his Web site on the screen.

I'd already figured out that a Web site is a kind of

24

billboard advertising the services of the millions of people who are connected via computer to the Internet. If someone is looking for a teacher to give him private language lessons, for example, he can access Mr John's Web site – among many others. When you bring up a Web site on the monitor, the first thing you see is the so-called home page, which generally displays the name of a person or firm and the services they provide. Often, there are one or more pages giving additional details.

Although Mr John had created one of these additional pages, he hadn't written anything on it. It was blank – or at least it had been.

Mr John proceeded to access this additional page. What appeared on the screen was:

The time has come.
Enrico and Caruso, the guinea pigs, have settled down at last, old William the tomcat has retired to his blanket for the night, and Mr John has gone out.
Now is the time to make a start on my life story. . .

Those were the opening words of my autobiography, the story of Freddy, the golden hamster that could read and write.

"Who wrote that?" demanded Mr John.

My reply couldn't have been shorter.

Me, I typed.

Mr John nodded. *Why?* he typed.

That couldn't have been shorter either – or longer, because Mr John's little *Why?* contained just about all he *could* have asked, like: why were you so irresponsible? Why would you put yourself at risk? Why endanger us all? Why did you have to go public with your life story? Why didn't you consult me first?

But, above all, that *Why?* boiled down to this: why did you break your promise?

I had faithfully sworn to Mr John not to tell a soul that I could read and write. Not even Sophie and her parents knew. I had solemnly raised my paw when I gave Mr John that assurance.

Although I'd known that I was breaking our agreement

when I typed my story on the Internet, I'd soothed my guilty conscience with a cop-out. Ashamed as I am to admit it, looking back, I tried that silly cop-out now.

But, I typed, *nobody knows it was me who wrote that stuff.*

That made Mr John hopping mad. His eyebrows positively bristled, and he snorted like a charging bull.

What do you take me for?! he pounded out on the keyboard. *At least own up to the mess you've got us into!* More calmly, he added: *And my Web site gives our address.*

I hung my head in shame.

And another thing, Mr John keyed in. *Forget about me and William and Enrico and Caruso, but how could you drag Sophie and her parents into this? You think*

*her mum will be pleased with what you wrote about her?
It was less than flattering. What if her friends read it?*

But, I ventured.

Mr John continued, *Get this into your thick head: a writer
doesn't describe people who exist in real life, he invents people
who could exist in real life.*

OK, SO I WASN'T A WRITER.

*We'll remove your story from the Web site, of course. Have you
saved it somewhere else?*

I nodded.

Well, keep it. It's pretty good.

Maybe I was a writer after all. *Thanks, Mr John,* I typed.

OK, kid, Mr John typed back. *Now let's drop the subject.*

It wasn't until he keyed in the last word that I realized
he'd been communicating with me via the Mac. He'd
settled matters between us in silence.

That meant William and Enrico and Caruso hadn't
heard a word of what was, from my point of view, a highly
embarrassing episode.

And I resolved to make sure they never found out.

CHAPTER FOUR

ENRICO AND CARUSO WERE through with their Sherlock Holmes act and had now gone into their "We're two quite normal guinea pigs" routine. They sat quietly on their straw, their beady little eyes darting from me to Sir William and back.

"Freddy, my friend," Sir William said softly, "have you any idea how Professor Fleischkopf could have found out about you?"

I raised an apologetic paw. "Not a clue, I'm afraid."

Sir William looked at Enrico and Caruso. "He's actually denying it."

"What?" I said innocently. I was feeling uneasy.

Caruso suddenly drew himself up. "Freddy, come here please!" I still don't know how he managed it, but he'd imitated Mr John's voice. "I've got a bone to pick with you."

I was staggered to see that Enrico had cowered down

in front of him like a picture of misery. More precisely, like a wretched little hamster.

"Is that good enough for you?" demanded Sir William. "Or shall we continue?"

I shook my head and stared at the floor. Somehow, it seemed the right thing to do just then.

"You tried to keep it a secret from us," Sir William went on. "And that, my dear Freddy, I find rather disappointing from an animal point of view. Anything to say in your defence?"

"No." I raised my head. "Except that I'm sorry." Sir William eyed me sharply, so I added, "Really sorry." Then he nodded.

"But how did you know what I'd posted on the Internet?" I couldn't resist asking. "I mean, none of you can read."

As though at a given signal, Enrico and Caruso jumped up, and I was startled to see them clamber out of their cage.

Enrico planted himself on my right and Caruso on my

left. "Shall we let you in on a secret?" Enrico whispered, putting his paw around me. "We can read perfectly well!"

"We can read what's in your heart," Caruso whispered, putting his paw around me from the other side. "We're like you, you see."

"We're artists: we're actors and mimes," Enrico said softly.

"And you're an artist too: a writer and a poet," Caruso added.

Lowering their voices still more, they whispered into my ears from either side:

31

"An actor with no audience
would stand there looking dumb.
A writer no one ever read
would never earn a crumb."

My heart warmed to them.

Enrico and Caruso understood what Mr John apparently had failed to grasp: my reason for putting my story on the Internet. A true writer writes for the benefit of other people – he needs a public. Those guinea pigs knew how I felt.

"Thank you, boys," I said. "That's what I call professional solidarity."

"In that case, I'm sure you'll also grant our request," said Enrico, and the two of them let go of me.

"What request?" I didn't like the sound of it.

"We want to conquer a new audience," Caruso explained. "Mr John, to be exact. We want to put on a musical for him."

"A musical?"

"Yes," said Enrico. "It'll get around the language problem. We'll whistle the tunes and type the lyrics on the Mac at the same time."

"Isn't that a brilliant idea?" said Caruso. "The only problem is, we can't write, as you know."

"Hence our request, Freddy: teach us to write." Enrico clasped his paws together in entreaty. "Please!"

MY HEART SANK.

I had a vivid mental picture of my nights at the computer in the not-too-distant future: Enrico and Caruso would hammer away at the keys and whistle their frightful tunes while I sat beside the keyboard, a melancholy outcast.

What if I refused? What if I turned them down? No, I couldn't do that. Everyone was entitled to an education, even a guinea pig. Farewell, then, you quiet nights at the keyboard – farewell to the delights of creative solitude. Feeling positively sick at heart, I turned away.

And then I heard a spluttering sound. I turned back to see Enrico and Caruso exploding with laughter. They squeaked and chortled, wrapping their paws around each other as if mutual support were all that prevented them from collapsing with mirth – which it probably was.

"If His Hamstership were wearing trousers," squeaked Enrico, "he'd have wet them by now."

"The great writer has made himself at home in his ivory tower," yelled Caruso, "and now the common folk, the riff-raff – in short, two guinea pigs – are trying to invade his privacy!"

Enrico assumed a sudden air of solemnity. "The only question is, do we really want to invade his privacy? Is admission to the great writer's ivory tower really so tempting? Methinks the price is a trifle too high, Caruso."

"It is, Enrico. Why should anyone with a mind to sing and whistle want to turn on a computer and manipulate the keys?"

Whereupon Enrico and Caruso began to sing – no, to raise the roof:

"For computers we've no time at all,
nor for keyboards nor modems nor RAM.
We prefer to create what we call
our own entertainment programme."

And they hugged each other once more, screeching with laughter.

They'd overdone it. I couldn't allow a pair of guinea pigs to subject the likes of me to such treatment. Still, I kept my cool. I calmly waited until Enrico and Caruso had stopped laughing, then waited a little longer.

I waited until they were staring at me curiously.

Then, all at once, I drew myself up, blew out my cheek pouches, and emitted a snarl – and they toppled. Enrico and Caruso simply fell over backwards with fright.

It works every time.

Those two are completely defenceless against a hamster's show of aggression, and the nice thing is, they keep forgetting about it. That's guinea pigs for you. On the other hand, I use this weapon sparingly, if only because Sir William accuses me of playing dirty. Today, however, even he seemed to agree that the two jokers deserved to be taught a little lesson.

"That's enough," was all he said. "Please behave yourselves. Have you forgotten how serious the situation is?" While they were scrambling to their feet, he went on, "We must have a discussion. What are we going to do if Professor Fleischkopf comes back and manages to break in?"

"That's easy," Caruso panted. "Freddy will scare him off."

"Exactly," said Enrico. "He'll blow out his cheeks and snarl."

Sir William shook his head reprovingly. "I'm being serious."

"So are we," said Caruso, and Enrico added, "Hamsters

36

are powerless against humans, that's what we were getting at."

When they were right, they were right.

But I said nothing. The whole conversation struck me as pointless because, unlike Sir William, I didn't actually believe that Professor Fleischkopf would manage to get into the apartment, judging by the way he'd bungled his first attempt.

Sir William was deep in thought. After a while he said, "What if we inform little Sophie? She'll be coming to feed us at noon tomorrow. If you write her a message, Freddy, she'll go and get her father. Gregory's a human – a big one too. A man like him should be able to deal with Professor Fleischkopf."

"But, Sir William," I said, "what about my promise to Mr John? No one's supposed to know I can write, not even Sophie. I gave him my word. I can't break it again, can I?"

No, I couldn't.

We came to that conclusion after a long debate (all the

longer because Enrico and Caruso played two gabby politicians for a change). Our decision: not a word to Sophie when she came to feed us tomorrow.

That, as it soon turned out, was a pretty disastrous mistake.

We also decided that, if Professor Fleischkopf *did* break into the apartment, I would simply hide.

That was another pretty disastrous mistake.

One mistake too many for a hamster in mortal danger.

And two too many for a girl named Sophie.

BeCAUSe NOW SHe, TOO, WAS IN DANGeR.

CHAPTER FiVE

I SAT AND WAITED for Sophie on Mr John's desk.

I always did that when she came visiting. That way, she got a good view of me wolfing down the mealworms she regularly brought me as a gift. (It's wonderful luck that mealworms taste delicious but go bad very quickly, because the question that always bothers an animal like me – "Should I save it or eat it right away?" – doesn't arise.)

It was early afternoon. Any moment now, I would hear light footsteps on the stairs, hear the key turn in the lock, and catch a whiff of Sophie's personal aroma (a wholesome and appetizing smell of sunflower seeds).

When my name is softly called,
when my little whiskers twitch,
when the scent of sunflower seeds
fills my nose and makes it itch,
when the mealworm in my mouth

melts like butter, when — oh dear,
stop it, Freddy, that's enough.
What it means is: Sophie's here!

I christened that poem "Afternoon Bliss", and in my personal opinion it's a prize example of sensitive, golden-hamsterish verse. The sad thing is, I can't show it to Sophie, or she'd know I can write. We're like two prisoners in adjoining cells, so near and yet so far. The gulf between hamsterdom and humankind is wide indeed.

So there I sat on the afternoon in question (it was the day after Professor Fleischkopf's attempt to break in), waiting for the sound of Sophie's footsteps on the stairs.

Sure enough, there she was, but not on her own. Accompanying her footsteps were those of two big, heavy grown-ups. Who could they be? If there had been only one other person, I'd have bet on Gregory, her father, but two?

The footsteps paused outside the front door. A key was inserted in the lock. It turned, and Sophie came dashing in, preceded by her usual scent of sunflower seeds.

"Freddy!" she cried.

Gregory followed her into the study, together with his pleasant personal odour of nutmeg. And behind Gregory came . . . **MUM!**

I'd been spared the sight of Mum ever since her hamster-hair allergy had banished me from the family home and got me transferred to Mr John's apartment. Spared the smell of her too. She sometimes smelled faintly of lavender, but mostly of tangy chervil. Today, for example, the study simply reeked of chervil.

She caught sight of me at once. "What's this? That creature is roaming around free!"

Sharp as a razor, Mum is.

"Here, Freddy." Sophie deposited a mealworm in front of me.

Thanks, Sophie, but I won't give you a welcoming wave, not today, or Mum will think I'm trying to butter her up.

"The air in here must be full of hamster hairs." Mum was holding a tissue over her nose and mouth. "I should have waited for you in the car."

41

You can say *that* again, Mum. There'd now be one more happy hamster in the world.

I decided to help Mum on her way. Taking the mealworm between my forepaws, I sat up as straight as I could, bared my teeth, and slowly and deliberately sank them into the worm. The fact that, when my teeth pierced the skin, some of the delicious guts spurted across the room was regrettable on the one hand, but intentional on the other.

"Ugh! How revolting!" Mum yelped. She turned on her heel. "I'm going downstairs!"

A record time for Mum-clearance, I'd say.

Anyway, she beat it so quickly, I was able to perform my welcoming wave for Sophie after all.

"That trick of his never ceases to amaze me." Gregory shook his head. "A hamster simply isn't designed for waving."

This one is, Gregory, as you can see.

But Gregory isn't a science teacher, he's a musician. More precisely, he plays the

trumpet. I know that only from hearsay, thank goodness, because the sound of a trumpet is poison to a hamster's sensitive ears. On the other hand, I'd have liked to know what kind of music he plays. For some reason, I've always pictured him playing a sad, Mexican trumpet solo like the one in the western Enrico and Caruso watched one time with Mr John. (The three of them sometimes watch TV at night, Mr John for relaxation and the guinea pigs to improve their acting technique – or so they say. Me, I'd rather read. As for Sir William, he prefers to lie on his blanket and meditate on world affairs – or so *he* says.)

"Let's be quick, Sophie," said Gregory. "We better not keep your mother waiting too long."

"Yes, Daddy," Sophie said obediently. She's a bit *too* obedient for my taste, but perhaps I'm prejudiced, being a freedom-loving hamster.

They doled out our food in double-quick time. They opened a can of cat food for Sir William, gave Enrico and Caruso plenty of carrots and lettuce, and I got my usual mixture of grain.

43

"OK," said Gregory, "that's taken care of. So long, the four of you."

"Daddy," Sophie said suddenly, "what if something bad happens? What if the place catches fire, for instance? They'd be trapped."

Gregory plucked at his moustache. "Hmm, you've got a point. Know what? We'll simply leave the door unlocked. If worst comes to worst, William can open it by pulling the handle down."

"And if a burglar breaks in?"

Gregory looked around. "No offence to John, but I hardly think there's anything here worth stealing."

Sophie gently stroked the fur on the nape of my neck. "See you tomorrow, Freddy."

See you tomorrow, Sophie.

See you tomorrow. . . That's what people say when they take it for granted nothing bad will happen in the meantime.

CHAPTER SIX

IT WAS AROUND TEN O'CLOCK that same night.

I wanted to finish off my horror story, "The Curse of the Weasel", before morning. First, however, to get my grey matter working and improve my capacity for thought, I went jogging on the hamster carousel in my cage.

The carousel is a circular wooden disc mounted on its axle at a slight angle, so it rotates when you run on it. Of course, I could also go jogging around the apartment, but I'd have to watch where I was going, not to mention avoiding Mr John's feet when he was at home. All of that would overtax my brain. On the hamster carousel I could jog and think at the same time.

So I went for a jog and tried to work out the ending of my story. What if I made the weasel go raving mad?

Sir William, if I remember correctly, was having a late-night snack while Enrico and Caruso were trying out a new series of tunes in their cage. They were whistling nice and quietly for a change.

Even so, I failed to hear the footsteps on the stairs.

Or rather, I paid no attention to them. A lone individual's footsteps would have alerted me, but these were the footsteps of two people – the couple who lived on the floor below, or so I assumed.

What first started me thinking was a smell – a strong smell I couldn't place immediately. Then I remembered how Mr John used to lubricate the rusty old typewriter he wrote with before he bought his computer: it was the smell of lubricating oil.

And then I suddenly detected another smell – one I recognized: SULPHUR! It was Professor Fleischkopf's antidandruff shampoo, and he was right outside our front door!

I wasted no time. Like greased lightning, I climbed out of the cage and on to the bookshelf, then down my little rope ladder to the floor, and ran to find Sir William.

He had already detected both smells. The speed with which he reacted – I must stress this – left little or nothing to be desired. "Quick, get lost!" he told me. "Behind the bathtub with you! I shall conceal myself in the clothes closet. Enrico and Caruso can take refuge under the chest of drawers."

The bathtub was a first-class idea – they'd have had to dismantle it completely in order to get at me. Hiding in the clothes closet and under the chest of drawers struck me as less favourable courses of action.

Click! went the front door.

Then came a faint creak as it opened.

"No problem, boss," I heard someone say. "A baby with two left hands could have got it open."

Footsteps.

Click! The front door had been closed from the inside.

"Honestly, boss." It was one of those deep, rumbling

male voices that sound pleasant at first but signal a
RED ALERT when you listen more closely. "Honestly,
boss, you could have handled this job by yourself."

"Nonsense, Brewster." That was *his* voice, the voice of
Professor Fleischkopf. "In the first place, stop calling me
'boss'. Secondly, I employed you to perform certain tasks.
One of which was to get that door open. The other is to
help me catch a golden hamster."

"Sure, OK, boss, say no more." A pause, then: "I still
don't get it, boss. Have we really broken into this joint to
snitch a hamster?"

"Once and for all, Brewster: I'm paying you to obey
orders, not to ask questions. And no lights," Fleischkopf
added. "Only flashlights."

"OK, OK, boss. Let's grab the animal's cage and beat
it." Footsteps, then: "There's the cage, but. . . Hey, the
little door's open. Looks like it's skedaddled."

"Very observant of you. And now, stop blathering and
start looking for it."

They searched everywhere.

I heard their footsteps, heard them combing the apartment, saw an occasional glimmer of light, and felt safe in my hideaway.

But my heart beat so hard, the tips of my whiskers quivered.

What was Professor Fleischkopf up to? Being an expert on rodents, he must have realized that an animal like me could find inaccessible hiding places. How did he hope to catch me anyway?

The closet door creaked open. Silence. Then it creaked again. Someone had shut it. Sir William must have escaped detection thanks to his jet-black fur.

I heard someone grunt. From the sound of it, the man named Brewster had gone down on his knees.

49

"Hey, I got something, boss! Two animals – they're hiding under the chest of drawers."

"Two? They must be Enrico and Caruso. Not interested."

"What? Who?"

"Enrico and – just two guinea pigs. They're of no scientific value. It's the hamster we're after."

"But, boss, guinea pigs are pretty much like hamsters. Let's grab 'em and beat it."

"Shut up!" Professor Fleischkopf's footsteps had paused in my vicinity. "In here, Brewster. In the bathroom!"

I made myself as flat as a pancake. Brewster came clomping in. I caught the flicker of a flashlight.

"Hmm." Professor Fleischkopf seemed to be deliberating. Suddenly he said, "Very well, we'll have to try a different tack."

Like what? What did he have in mind?

I listened tensely. Then I heard:

"I'm now going to say something, and I'd advise you to take it very seriously."

"Er. . . Who do you mean, boss?"

"*Ssh!* We're going now."

"Why, boss? We haven't caught the creature yet."

"Shut up, Brewster! We're going now, but we'll be back tomorrow night. And then – *then* you'll give yourself up." Professor Fleischkopf inserted a pause. "If you don't, a certain young lady will be in great danger. A young lady named Sophie."

Silence.

After a while Brewster said, "Boss, are you feeling OK? I mean, what's all this about a young lady?"

"For the last time, Brewster, shut up! I know what I'm doing."

"Are you sure, boss? I mean, really sure?"

"Come on, Brewster, we're going."

"To be honest, boss, that's fine with me."

They left the bathroom, and I heard their footsteps recede in the direction of the front door.

There I sat in my hideaway behind the bathtub, faced with a considerable problem.

At the same time, I knew how to solve it. When Sophie came tomorrow, I would have to use the computer after all.

"Oh, one more thing," I heard Professor Fleischkopf say suddenly. "Please listen carefully. I feel sure your ears are sharp enough to identify the following noise."

The noise was an unpleasant, metallic scraping sound, followed by a kind of PLOP!

It sounded like an electric plug being extracted from an outlet.

And naturally, there was only one plug it could be.

Professor Fleischkopf had disconnected the Mac!

CHAPTER SEVEN

I SAT ON THE DESK AND WAVED.

I waved desperately.

There were no two ways about it: my despair was definitely on the rise. To be absolutely frank, I'd seldom felt so miserable – so utterly and completely helpless.

Not that it had begun like that. "My dear Freddy," Sir William said soothingly when I ran over to him after Professor Fleischkopf and Brewster had gone, "none of *us* can stick that plug in again, that's obvious, but little Sophie could. You shouldn't find it difficult to make it clear to her what she has to do."

No, of course not. Suddenly, I couldn't think why I'd got so worked up.

I wasn't worked up even now, as I waved to Sophie.

I was simply desperate.

Needless to say, I didn't just wave any old way. I made some highly meaningful gestures designed to tell Sophie what I wanted her to do. Those gestures had one little disadvantage: she didn't understand what they meant.

"It's all right, Freddy," she said. Then she laughed. "Take it easy now." Then, sounding slightly impatient, "I said it's all right, Freddy!"

I GAVE UP. I HAD FAILED.

"Oh dear, Caruso," I heard suddenly. "Seems like the great writer has developed a communication problem."

"It's worse than that, Enrico — it's the very worst thing that can happen to any writer. He's got a potential reader, but nothing to write with."

Enrico and Caruso were sitting underneath the desk. Sophie, who couldn't hear them, hadn't noticed them yet.

"What does that tell us?" asked Enrico, breaking into verse. "Deprived of any way to write, a writer soon gives up the fight."

Caruso continued, "If writing cannot fill the bill, the art of mime both can and will."

Sir William had strolled up. "They'd like to take a shot at it. You'll let them, Freddy, won't you?"

Seated overhead on the edge of the desk, I could only nod.

The guinea pigs set to work. They began by uttering their usual shrill whistles, which hurt my ears but instantly attracted Sophie's attention.

"Hey, you two," she said, "I've already fed you."

Enrico and Caruso darted over to the wall, where the Mac's plug was lying loose on the floor.

I have to admit it: what those guinea pigs did next was incredibly simple but incredibly successful.

Caruso grabbed the electric cable in his mouth, just behind the plug, and went over to the outlet, where Enrico, who had sat up on his haunches, was pointing to it with both forepaws.

Sophie caught on at once.

55

"You want me to stick in the plug?" she asked. Caruso nodded vigorously, Enrico pointed and whistled like a maniac.

Sophie looked down at them with a thoughtful expression. She was probably wondering why two guinea pigs would want a computer reconnected to the power.

Suddenly she shook her head. "No," she said, "I can't do that." Another pause for thought. "If Mr John took the plug out, he must have had his reasons. I'd better leave it that way."

Running away wasn't as hard as I'd thought.

It was a whole lot harder.

Our escape from Mr John's apartment nearly ended at the top of the stairs, at least where Enrico and Caruso were concerned.

"I don't dare!" Caruso was clinging to the edge of the top step, several paw's-breadths from the next one down.

Enrico, standing just below, was bracing himself

against Caruso's fat butt. "Come on, let go," he panted. "I'll break your fall."

"Promise?"

"Cross my heart."

Caruso let go. He landed on top of Enrico with a thud, burying his scrawny friend beneath him.

"Get off me," Enrico gasped. "I can't breathe!"

Caruso rolled aside, and Enrico scrambled to his feet.

Breathing heavily, the two of them peered over the edge of the next step down. "Oh no," Caruso groaned, "there must be dozens of them. How on earth are we going to make it to the bottom?"

How indeed? That was exactly why I'd been against taking Enrico and Caruso along in the first place.

✳ ✳ ✳

We'd assembled for a council of war as soon as Sophie had departed with a cheerful, "See you tomorrow!" It was not long (this time, Enrico and Caruso assumed the role of keen, decisive businessmen) before two things became clear.

First, I couldn't afford to remain in the apartment.

Second, it was absolutely essential for Professor Fleischkopf to learn of my escape. Only that would convince him that his plan wasn't working, and that his threat to harm Sophie had lost its point.

But where should I take refuge? On the roof, which I might have to share with a flock of scruffy pigeons? In the cellar, with a host of spiders and bugs? On the street, dodging dogs and automobiles? Or should I set off into the unknown, where it might be dirty or cold or noisy or all three at once?

Of course not. I would naturally take refuge somewhere safe, clean, warm, and peaceful. And, moreover, where there was plenty of food. I would hide away in Sophie and Gregory's apartment. (Mum's hamster-hair allergy was a problem I'd solve when I got there, not before. "Never oil a hamster's tread-wheel until it starts squeaking," as Great-Grandmother used to say.) I had already made several trips between the family's apartment and our own, though always in a closed container. However, I relied on my sense of direction to recognize the route (we hamsters can find our way through an elaborate pitch-black system of tunnels that make the Minotaur's legendary labyrinth look like a straight, brightly illuminated footpath). One thing was certain: I could escape only under cover of darkness, not in broad daylight through streets thronged with people.

"Next item on the agenda:" – Caruso pretended to check off something on a list – "Freddy is so small, he'll never make it on foot. How's he going to get there?"

There was only one answer. I had a tried-and-true means of getting to places I couldn't reach by myself. But the animal in question naturally had to be consulted. "Sir William," I said politely, "would it be asking too much if I begged a ride on your back?"

Sir William looked at me. "To be honest, my friend — yes, it would. I haven't left this apartment since I was a kitten. Am I now, at my advanced age, expected to venture not only down the stairs and out of the house but through a succession of crowded streets? Expected to do that, moreover, with a hamster's teeth buried in the back of my neck — teeth that can sometimes, I might add, inflict a nasty nip?"

Sir William paused. "Very well, I merely wanted to state that for the record. Of course I'll give you a lift, Freddy. That goes without saying."

"Thank you," I said, wondering yet again why Sir William behaves as if he is as old as Great-Grandmother. According to my calculations he's in the prime of his life. But maybe that's just it. Sir William is a civilized feline, as he calls it. In plain English, he's been neutered, and neutered tomcats probably feel older than their age.

"Let's get going." Enrico pretended to check off another item on a list. "Next comes the sixty-four-thousand-dollar question: how will Professor Fleischkopf learn of Freddy's escape?"

To be honest, I didn't know. Even if I disappeared from the apartment, Professor Fleischkopf would think I was still hiding there. That meant he'd do precisely what he hoped would lure me out: he'd take Sophie hostage.

Sir William shook his massive head. "I'm surprised you even asked that question, Enrico. The answer's as plain as the paw in front of your face. Professor Fleischkopf will realize Freddy's gone if we *all* disappear, not just Freddy."

I might have thought of that myself, to be frank. Perhaps it hadn't occurred to me because the idea had a considerable drawback.

"But that would mean that Enrico and Caruso must come too," I said.

Sir William smiled faintly. "Sometimes, my dear Freddy, your powers of deduction are positively breathtaking."

"I only meant to point out that it'll turn my escape

into a kind of mass exodus," I said, controlling myself with an effort.

"We'd be happy to stay behind," Enrico volunteered. "After all, we've nothing to fear from Professor Fleischkopf."

"Quite right," said Caruso. "We're of no scientific value; he said so himself."

But it wouldn't work without them, I realized that. To my humiliation, they then insisted on receiving an express invitation from me to join the party.

Caruso gave me a condescending pat on the back. "You've made the right decision, Freddy. Who knows? Maybe we can make ourselves useful on the journey."

Make themselves useful? THOSE TWO?

BaH!

✳ ✳ ✳

So there I sat, perched on the back of Sir William's neck, waiting for Enrico and Caruso instead of making a beeline for Sophie and Gregory's apartment. They had got into an argument on the second step down.

"Not that again!" Enrico complained in rhyme. "I'm far too small."

"I need something," Caruso retorted indignantly, "to break my fall."

"Your fat backside should do the trick."

"Maybe, but frankly, I'm scared sick."

"Let's jump when I count up to three."

"There's naught else for it, I can see."

In my estimation, that said it all. Enrico counted to three and the two of them landed with a thud on the step below. They got up, groaning, and tackled the next one. I tried to keep my cool, but it would obviously be quite a

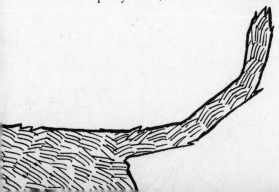

while before they reached the door to the street. I could feel Sir William growing fidgety beneath me.

What if one of the neighbours suddenly appeared? What if someone turned on the stairwell light and discovered us? What would we do then?

Nothing. More precisely, we would simply hunker down and hope for the best. "We can't allow for every contingency," Sir William had said. "We'll need a little luck as well." Fine, except that it looked as if a little luck wouldn't be enough.

We were blessed with it after all, that extra smidgen of luck we needed. It held out until we reached the door to the street.

Enrico and Caruso were just tackling the third step from the bottom when I scented something.

Faint but perceptible, it was coming from outside.

A smell of sulphur and lubricating oil.

CHAPTER EIGHT

"LOOK OUT!" I CRIED. "Professor Fleischkopf and Brewster – they're coming!"

Sir William had already smelled them. With a mighty leap, he reached the front door and flattened himself against the wall. "Here, quick!" he called to Enrico and Caruso. "We must all be behind the door when they open it!"

I couldn't see them in the gloomy hallway, but it seemed to me they were hesitating. "Hurry!" I yelled. "Jump! Come on, jump!"

There were two dull thuds, followed by agonized squeaks and a patter of feet. The guinea pigs were making a terrible racket. Unlike our previous cries in Interanimal, it was audible to human ears as well.

"*Ssh!* Just a moment!" I heard Professor Fleischkopf say. "What was that?"

"What was what, boss?"

"It sounded like. . . All right, come on, and be quiet!"

"No need to tell *me* that, boss. I'm a pro."

The front door opened just as Enrico and Caruso darted into our corner and flattened themselves against the skirting board, breathing heavily.

The beam of a flashlight roamed across the hallway and lingered at the bottom of the stairs.

"Odd," muttered the Professor. "I could have sworn I heard something."

"Well, I didn't. What do you think it was, boss?"

"Nothing. Forget it. Come on!"

"Quick!" I whispered. "Out the door and into the street!"

The front door had just begun to close. Sir William and I made it through in a flash. Enrico dashed out almost simultaneously. As for Caruso, he made it by a whisker. The door slammed shut just behind him.

"Really, Brewster!" I heard Professor Fleischkopf say inside. "I told you to be quiet!"

"Take it easy, boss. You're paying me to open doors, not close them."

The Professor growled something unintelligible, and then I heard the two of them start up the stairs.

"What now?" I asked Sir William. I have to admit I couldn't get my bearings at first. Although it was somewhat lighter outside than in the hallway, I could see precious little. Hamsters are notorious for their poor eyesight (there are still no hamster glasses on the market, by the way). I could smell, but there was such a bewildering mixture of scents that my nose was no help either – not to mention my ears. Far from it. I tried to shut them to blot out the noise of the traffic, which I found quite deafening.

"Over there!" Sir William jerked his head at a dark, looming bush. "Let's hide in there for now. Hang on tight with your teeth, Freddy!" He leaped off the stone steps that led up to the front door and burrowed his way beneath the overhanging vegetation. Enrico and Caruso hesitated again. I was seriously beginning to doubt if we would ever get to Sophie and Gregory's apartment. Then the two of them finally mustered the courage and jumped off the steps. They landed heavily in the front yard, the impact coinciding with a suppressed squeak. Had one of them injured himself? Apparently not, because they crawled beneath the bush and joined us.

Not a moment too soon.

I heard Professor Fleischkopf and Brewster come storming back down the stairs. Then the front door was wrenched open.

"Those dastardly creatures!" hissed the Professor, beside himself with fury. "I knew it! It must have been them I heard, and now, of course, they've got clean away. I can even guess where they're headed: that little girl's place. If only I knew her address!"

"Don't panic, boss, they couldn't have gone too far. Know what we'll do?"

"No, but I'm sure you'll tell me."

"I'm going to fetch my dog. He'll track those critters down in no time."

"Your dog?"

"Sure, boss. Rex only has to look at a cat and it drops dead."

"Is that so? Good, but he musn't harm the hamster, not on any account."

"Don't worry, boss. Rex only has a thing about cats."

They hurried off.

Sir William extricated himself from the bush. "Let's get out of here! Where to, Freddy?"

"Head in the opposite direction." I had more or less got my bearings by now, but. . .

A plaintive voice came from the depths of the bush. "I've sprained my right hind paw. I can't walk on it." Who else but Caruso?

Enrico crawled out of the undergrowth. "You two keep going. We'll follow you."

Sir William sighed – quite loudly too. "Very decent of you, but absolutely crazy. You have no idea which way to go, you can't get back into the apartment, and Brewster will soon be back with that mutt of his. What are we going to do? This is a genuine emergency. . . Wait a minute!" He straightened up. "Even a three-legged cat can catch mice if he's hungry enough, as my late father used to say. OF COURSE! *That's* what we'll do."

Professor Fleischkopf and Brewster were back within a quarter of an hour. The dog's hoarse barking could be heard from a long way off. Sir William peered out of the bush. Then he hurriedly withdrew his head. "Good heavens! How frightful! That Rex animal is a regular monster." He gave a sudden smile. "All the better. It may work," he said – mysteriously, because he hadn't breathed a word about what he was planning. "Keep an eye on the time, my friends, that's all. Our arrangement still stands."

All we'd arranged was that we would wait a good hour for Sir William to return. "If I'm not back by then, you'll have to manage on your own."

The hoarse barking drew nearer. Sir William squared

his shoulders. "This is it! Wish me luck." And away he went. I peered out cautiously.

My eyes had now grown so accustomed to the darkness, I could make out the animal that Brewster was towing by its leash along the pavement. It was a fearsome cross between a German shepherd and a mastiff — a monster whose foot-long tongue protruded from between two rows of fangs that would have graced a sabre-toothed tiger. Behind Brewster, and at a respectful distance from the dog, came Professor Fleischkopf.

Sir William was nowhere to be seen.

Suddenly, though, I heard his voice.

"YOO-HOO, REX!"

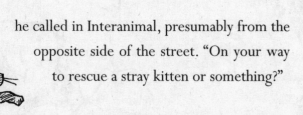

he called in Interanimal, presumably from the opposite side of the street. "On your way to rescue a stray kitten or something?"

"*What!?*" Rex stopped short. Tongue lolling, he glared in the direction of Sir William's voice.

"Behold the mighty friend and protector of pussycats, engaged on another mercy mission. Good boy, Rex."

"What *is* all this hooey?!" Rex barked in Interanimal. "Who says I'm a cat lover?"

"Oh, everyone does," Sir William said suavely. "Me, for one."

"That's a lousy lie!" Rex started tugging at his leash again. "Show yourself, you liar! Come on out, you coward!"

"With pleasure." Sir William emerged from behind a rubbish bin on the opposite pavement.

He came prancing out like a ballet dancer and continued to caper

around as he chanted the following words like a child taunting a playmate: "Rexy is a cat lover! Rexy is a cat lover!"

That was too much for Rex. With one gigantic leap, he wrenched the leash out of Brewster's hand and charged across the street, barking madly. Sir William promptly disappeared into the mouth of a garage. There must have been a way through to the backyards beyond the houses, because Rex's barking quickly faded.

Brewster just stood there, rigid with bewilderment. "Rex!" he called. "Here, Rex! Heel, Rex! Come back!"

"Forget it, he's out of earshot," said Professor Fleischkopf. "Well done, Brewster," he added sarcastically. "Excellent work. You know which cat that was?"

"The one from the apartment?"

"The very same, Brewster, the very same."

"Rex is bound to catch him. Then I'll set him on our friend the hamster. We'll get them all, boss, you'll see."

"Let's hope so." The two men crossed the street. "Just

in case you've forgotten, Brewster: you don't get paid unless I see some results." And off they went in pursuit.

"Wow!" said Enrico beside me. "That was pretty cool."

"I wouldn't have thought it of Sir William," said Caruso.

"Sir William?" said a voice behind us. "Is that the tom-cat's name?"

We spun around.

Sitting behind us was a rat.

CHAPTER NINE

A SEWER RAT AT LEAST THE SIZE of Caruso, it had shaggy grey fur and unpleasantly sharp yellow teeth.

Hurriedly, I drew myself up and blew out my cheek pouches.

But the rat made a dismissive gesture.

"Relax," it said, "I don't feel like fighting." It grinned. "Anyway, you'd lose."

Which was true, unfortunately, though I now noticed that this rat was a lady rat. She seemed quite young and was probably an inexperienced fighter, but OK, I didn't feel like getting bitten either.

"My name's Freddy," I said, "and these are Enrico and Caruso."

"I'm Karen Greywhisker of Generation K," the girl rat said. "Hi, boys."

"Generation K?" I said.

"In our tribe, all the rats who are born around the same time get given names that start with the letter corresponding to their generation. That's why I'm called Karen, because K is the eleventh letter of the alphabet. Just between us rodents, though, it doesn't matter who's born when or where. What matters is the tribe, right?"

"I guess so," I said. I'd never had a conversation with a rat. It obviously posed problems to which a hamster wasn't quite equal. I glanced at Enrico and Caruso, but all they did was sit and stare.

"A fascinating subject," I went on politely. "The individual and his relationship to society – very interesting."

"Pooh," she said, "sociology bores me. But that tomcat of yours, *him* I find interesting. He's really cool, except that. . ." She wrinkled her nose, which made her whiskers bristle even more than usual. "What's he doing, hanging out with you rodents? There must be something wrong with him."

"Ah," I said, "that's because he's a civilized tomcat."

"Civilized?" Karen Greywhisker wrinkled her nose still more. Suddenly her face lit up. "Oh, you mean he's a pussycat."

"You're right in principle," I began, "but—"

At that moment Sir William dived beneath the bush. "Hello, folks!" he cried. "That was a breeze!" He was as chirpy as a chipmunk and looked years younger. "I shinned up a tree. Then, while Rex was barking down below, I jumped on to the one next door, climbed down, and here I am. That stupid mutt is still barking up the wrong tree!"

"But not for much longer," said Karen Greywhisker.

"*Grrr!*" Sir William arched his back and bristled all over. I'd never seen him do that before. Karen retreated, baring her teeth.

"Stop!" I cried. "Stop, Sir William! Take it easy, this is a friendly rodent."

Sir William regained control over his alarm system as quickly as it had activated itself. "I apologize, young lady, it's these tiresome reflexes of mine. On the other hand, where would we be without them?"

"Right on!" Karen showed her teeth again, this time in a grin. "Bite first, ask questions later – that's the Greywhisker philosophy."

I introduced the two of them. Then Karen said, "You're in a bind, boys." She pointed to Caruso. "You won't get far, not with Fatso and his sprained paw."

"Certainly not with Rex on our heels," Sir William agreed. "I'm out of ideas, I admit. What should we do?"

"What indeed?" Karen wrinkled her nose. She was obviously pondering the question. "We might think of something."

"You mean you've got an idea?" I asked hopefully.

"No," she said, "not me, but we Greywhiskers never do

anything on our own. The whole tribe may be able to work something out. Including Greywhisker the Great, of course."

"Greywhisker the Great? Is that your father?"

"Maybe, maybe not." Karen shrugged her shoulders. "He's our tribal chief, anyway." She looked at Sir William. "It'd be a shame if that stupid hound caught you." She wrinkled her nose again. "Very well, I'll take you down to where we live. The sewer, I mean."

I looked first at Sir William, then at Enrico and Caruso. None of them seemed eager to crawl through a smelly sewer, but what choice did we have?

At that moment, as if to speed us on our way, a flurry of barking rang out in the distance.

Karen Greywhisker briefed us on the way. "The boss can be a bit sarcastic, but he's got a heart of gold."

A heart of gold, bah! Those were the words of a daughter who idolized her daddy, even if he was only

a maybe-daddy. Then again, what about her continual references to "we" and "us" and "the tribe"? If the truth be told, they all boiled down to Greywhisker the Great himself.

I was not only miffed but feeling more and more so.

My well-devised escape plan, which should have transported me, riding swiftly and in comfort on Sir William's back, to the peace and cleanliness of Sophie's home, had degenerated into a trek along stinking, slimy tunnels awash with sewage.

I glanced back at Enrico and Caruso, who were

wading through a pool of sludge. It served them right! Still, they seemed to be in good spirits. While limping along (he did so remarkably briskly on his three good legs), Caruso whispered something to Enrico. They looked at each other, then giggled the way they normally did when cooking up some new theatrical performance – not that there could be any question of one right now.

Karen went on with her briefing, which she addressed exclusively to Sir William. "Greywhisker the Great isn't just our tribal chief, of course. He's the boss of our firm as well."

"Your firm?"

"Yes. Greywhisker & Sons & Daughters, Inc., Garbage Processors. We trade with other tribes of rats."

"Very interesting," said Sir William. "And how is business?"

"Not bad. It's a tricky job, sorting garbage. You need a sensitive nose and a good head for business – and those the boss most certainly has."

I saw Enrico and Caruso nod upon hearing those words. Why, I wondered, should it interest them that Greywhisker the Great was a smart businessman?

"Know something?" Karen said to Sir William. "I'm going to tell the boss how you bamboozled that dog. It'll make him look at you with different eyes."

"It might not be a bad idea," I put in, "if you also informed him that Professor Fleischkopf is after me in particular. After *me*!" I added, stressing the last word.

Karen gave me a cursory glance. "You can tell him yourself." She turned back to Sir William. "When you're checked by our security people, I'll naturally have to tell them you're a — what was the word? Oh yes, that's right — a *civilized* tomcat. They'd never let you into our rat's nest otherwise. It was really cool the way you fooled that stupid mutt."

Her flattery of Sir William had begun to get on my nerves, and by now i was feeling thoroughly low.

"The pussycat and the three mouse-keteers!" Greywhisker the Great roared with laughter. "On the way to see their queen, eh, what?!"

Well, Karen had warned us that he could be sarcastic.

Sir William smiled. "A strange but not uninteresting way of looking at our escape," he said politely. If the word *pussycat* had hurt his feelings, he showed no sign of it. His self-control was absolute.

I don't know how big sewer rats can become, but Greywhisker the Great was three times my height when sitting on his haunches. In my opinion, that should be the absolute maximum for any rat that expects to be classified as a member of the rodent family. His greyish-brown fur was as bristly as an old scrub brush but remarkably clean.

I'd always thought that sewer rats were dirty creatures, but the other rats clustered around us, though not exactly dapper, were also surprisingly clean. Moreover, the underground chamber in which we were sitting (evidently the tribe's assembly room) had been excavated with considerable skill. It was as damp as a stalactite cave, however, and I would never get my fur dry down there. If I didn't want to catch a bad case of pneumonia, I would have to regain the open air as soon as possible. Except that Professor Fleischkopf was lying

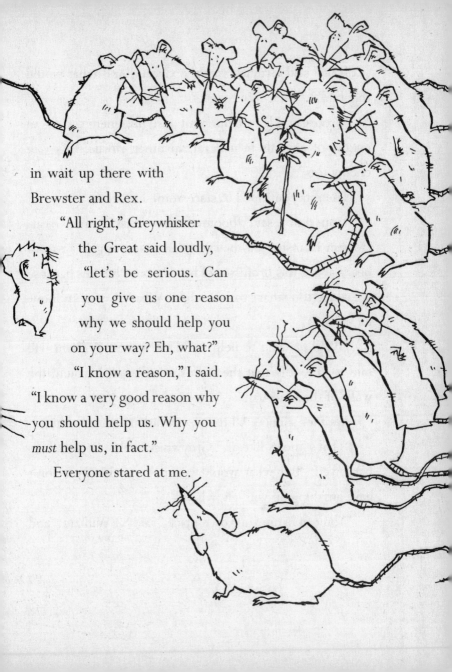

in wait up there with
Brewster and Rex.

"All right," Greywhisker
the Great said loudly,
"let's be serious. Can
you give us one reason
why we should help you
on your way? Eh, what?"

"I know a reason," I said.
"I know a very good reason why
you should help us. Why you
must help us, in fact."

Everyone stared at me.

"Oh?" said Greywhisker the Great. "And what would that be?"

"Professor Fleischkopf isn't just my enemy. He's an enemy of animals in general. In other words, he's *your* enemy too."

The rats continued to stare at me in silence.

"You don't say!" boomed Greywhisker the Great. "Master Hamster may be right, but we don't give a row of beans about this professor of his. He can't hurt us because we're far too smart to be caught. What do you say now, eh, what?"

"We'll *pay* you to help us!" That was Sir William. He said it so loudly that the words reverberated around the walls of the chamber.

Another silence. All the Greywhiskers stared at him.

"That's more like it." Greywhisker the Great's eyes narrowed. "But what would you pay us with? You don't have anything on you, eh, what?"

"You can name your own price," said Sir William, "and

we'll pay you as soon as we're out of danger. I give you my word of honour as a feline gentleman."

"Your word of honour, eh?" Greywhisker the Great surveyed his tribe. Then he said, "If you were a rat, we could accept it. But as things stand. . ."

At that moment, Enrico and Caruso stepped forward. They drew themselves up to their full height so that the whole tribe could see them.

"We've got a deal for you!"
they chorused.

All the Greywhiskers craned their necks.

Enrico and Caruso scanned the tribe. "We'll put on a show for you." They paused for effect. "And you'll help us in return." Another pause. "But only if you enjoy it."

CHAPTER TEN

IT TOOK ME A LITTLE WHILE to register what they had said.

A show! Those half-demented guinea pigs were actually offering to put on a show for the Greywhiskers! What did it mean, anyway, a "show"? I guessed it was a term they'd recently coined to describe their theatrical antics. And they expected the rats to help us in return for *that*?!

Hey, just a minute! I stiffened.

What was the other thing they'd said? "But only if you enjoy it." WHaT aBSOLUTE FOLLY! How could those crazy guinea pigs have made our survival dependent on whether or not the Greywhiskers enjoyed their show?

Easy, Freddy, calm down. Nothing was settled yet. I looked at Greywhisker the Great. An astute businessman like him would never agree to such a risky deal.

Greywhisker the Great said nothing. He stared at Enrico and Caruso in silence, plucking at his whiskers.

Suddenly he straightened up. "Done!" he said. "It's a deal."

I couldn't believe my ears.

Had He Gone Mad too?

Then I saw him smile complacently. Of course! He couldn't have made a better bargain. Businesswise, there wasn't the

slightest risk from his point of view. He was in a win-win situation, so to speak. When the show was over, all the Greywhiskers had to say was, "Sorry, folks, we didn't enjoy it" – and that would be that.

Enrico and Caruso requested fifteen minutes in which to get ready. Well, naturally: the stars had to prepare for their performance. Maybe there was a make-up artist somewhere around to daub them with greasepaint.

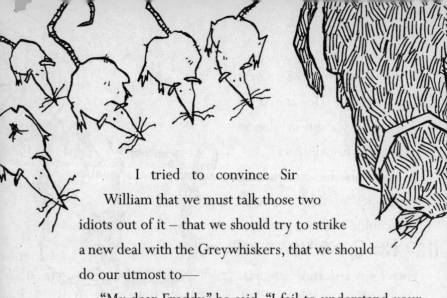

I tried to convince Sir William that we must talk those two idiots out of it – that we should try to strike a new deal with the Greywhiskers, that we should do our utmost to—

"My dear Freddy," he said, "I fail to understand your agitation. Are you scared the show won't be a success? Well, I'm not."

True, how could I have forgotten? His Lordship was a firm believer in the guinea pigs' theatrical talents. Except, unfortunately, he was no expert on the theatre.

What was more, Enrico and Caruso had always yearned to appear in front of a large audience. Those two conceited rodents would have sold their own grandmother for such an opportunity.

The show began.

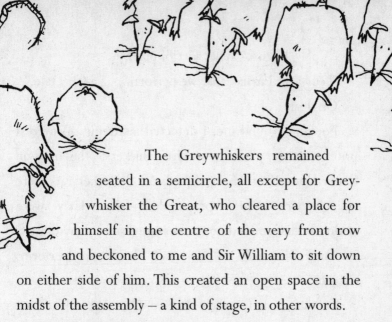

The Greywhiskers remained seated in a semicircle, all except for Greywhisker the Great, who cleared a place for himself in the centre of the very front row and beckoned to me and Sir William to sit down on either side of him. This created an open space in the midst of the assembly – a kind of stage, in other words.

Enrico and Caruso came on.

They walked quite normally (discounting the fact that Caruso was limping a little).

"What shall we give them, Caruso?" asked Enrico. He didn't shout or screech, just spoke in his usual voice.

"Let's put on a play, Enrico." Caruso's voice, too, sounded normal.

"A play, Caruso? What sort of play?"

"I suggest, Enrico, that we perform . . . a fairy tale."

Oh dear. . .

Looking around me, I detected a stirring of interest among the very youngest Greywhiskers – the ones in Generations N or M, I guessed. All the other rats were sitting there with expressionless faces. They were obviously determined not to be impressed by anything.

"And what sort of fairy tale should we perform, Caruso?"

"A guinea-pig fairy tale, Enrico. One that tells of love and deadly danger."

OH DEAR, OH DEAR, OH DEAR. . .

A guinea-pig fairy tale? The faces of the Greywhisker tribe had turned to stone. One thing was clear: after this introduction, Enrico and Caruso could perform whatever came into their heads, but they were doomed to fail.

And Sir William? He was smiling, though his smile

struck me as a bit strained. Perhaps it was dawning on him that his favourite actors were about to ruin our chances of survival.

"Well then, Caruso, let's begin."

Forget it, boys. Your efforts will be wasted.

Caruso sat down in the middle of the stage and began to speak. He did so in Interanimal, of course, but in a way that seemed to make his disembodied voice float in mid-air. It was like listening to a ventriloquist. A voice could be heard, but it didn't appear to be coming from Caruso.

Once upon a time, said the voice, *there was a guinea-pig king named Marmaduke the Mighty. He had many daughters, but his favourite was Princess Gwendoline. She was so beautiful that the stars themselves said, "Princess Gwendoline is the loveliest of all." Marmaduke the Mighty summoned her to his side every day, for he loved her dearly.*

While the voice continued to narrate, Enrico and Caruso began to act. Caruso played Marmaduke the Mighty and Enrico impersonated Gwendoline. Comfortably settled in his favourite chair with little Gwendoline on his lap, Marmaduke gladly submitted to her hugs and kisses. It was such a homey, affectionate scene, I couldn't help feeling rather moved.

From time to time, the voice went on, *Gwendoline left the safety of their burrow and went to play outside or look for things to eat. Her devoted father didn't like this, because all manner of dangers were lurking out there. But his little daughter reassured him.*

"I am always very careful, Daddy," squeaked Gwendoline, alias Enrico. Then she left the burrow for the sunny meadow above ground, and we saw her romping around amid the wild flowers and tasty herbs that grew there.

I stole a furtive glance at the others. The Greywhiskers were gazing at little Gwendoline with rapt attention, silently revelling in this delightful scene. Even Greywhisker the Great was wearing a rather dreamy expression.

But there were bad people around in those days — scientists who caught guinea pigs and subjected them to horrific medical experiments.

All at once, Caruso appeared in a different role. He stood up straight in spite of his injured leg, looking as tall and strong as a man. Little Gwendoline failed to notice him. He crept steadily closer, but still she went on nibbling herbs and sniffing flowers.

"Watch out!" I heard someone behind me hiss. Other rats joined in, and one Greywhisker actually called out, in a low voice, "Careful! There's a human just behind you!"

The scientist suddenly pounced on little Gwendoline and grabbed her by the scruff of the neck. She squeaked with terror, but it was no use. Having tied her up securely, he left her lying there. He was going off, he announced loudly, to fetch his surgical instruments.

Cut to Marmaduke the Mighty, who had settled down in his chair, quite unaware of what had happened.

But little Gwendoline's capture had not gone unnoticed.

Marmaduke the Mighty now received a visit from Enrico, whose bulging cheek pouches made it abundantly clear that he was playing a hamster.

"King Marmaduke," said the hamster, "I just saw a man

capture your daughter, Princess Gwendoline. I don't feel capable of rescuing her on my own, but the two of us could."

"Nonsense," said King Marmaduke. "My daughter Gwendoline is far too careful to let herself be caught. You're a hamster – you don't know much about guinea pigs. The animal the man caught was probably a rat."

"It *was* your daughter," the hamster insisted. "But even if it were a rat, shouldn't we try to rescue it?"

"I'm a guinea pig," said King Marmaduke. "What do I care about rats?"

Suddenly we were back with little Gwendoline, who was lying there tied up, the scientist at work beside her. He sharpened his scalpel, checked that his scissors were sharp, and prepared to embark on one of his horrific medical experiments. Scene change.

The hamster was still trying to convince Marmaduke the Mighty that even a rat deserved help, but Marmaduke merely kept repeating, "I'm a guinea pig, what do I care about rats?" So the hamster gave up. Sadly, he bade the guinea-pig king farewell.

Now things got really serious. The scientist raised his scalpel and little Gwendoline screamed terribly, but no one came to her aid.

The rats around me had risen to their feet. Some hissed, others booed, many chewed their forepaws in excitement, and Greywhisker the Great was fiercely plucking at his whiskers.

Another scene change.

Marmaduke the Mighty still sat in his favourite chair but looked less confident than before. Something was troubling him. Then we heard his inner voice.

King Marmaduke, said the dis-embodied voice from somewhere

overhead, *mightn't it be your little daughter Gwendoline after all? Are you willing to risk her life, just because you wouldn't help a rat?*

"No!" cried Marmaduke the Mighty. And he dashed out of the burrow and into the meadow, where he found little Gwendoline lying tied up on the ground (for some reason, her human tormentor had disappeared). Having severed the cords that bound her (with his teeth), he clasped her in his arms.

"Daddy!" cried she.

"Gwendoline! My favourite daughter!" cried he. And they wept with joy and relief.

So did the Greywhiskers around me.

I wouldn't have believed that sewer rats could shed tears, but they did. They sobbed and snivelled, howled and wailed, bawled and blubbered, many of them clasping their faces with their paws.

Big fat tears were trickling down Greywhisker the Great's cheeks.

"Freddy," he said hoarsely, "we'll help you." He draped a paw around my shoulders. "I get the point. We'll not only help you, but we'll do so for free."

What do you mean, for free? I felt tempted to say. You've just been paid. But Sir William gave an ever-so-slight shake of the head, so I held my tongue.

In any case, I was becoming preoccupied with an entirely different matter: I was freezing cold. My fur was still damp and would never dry out down here.

The rats couldn't do anything about the damp, and up above, where it was nice and dry, Professor Fleischkopf would still be lying in wait with Brewster and Rex.

I suddenly realized that, whatever the Greywhiskers did to help us, it would be a long time before this business was over.

And by then I'd be sick. And a sick hamster – Great-Grandmother had impressed on us – is as good as a dead hamster.

I STARTED TO SHIVER WITH COLD AND FEAR.

CHAPTER ELEVEN

I BLINKED IN THE SUNLIGHT.

It was streaming in through a very grimy window, but several of the panes were missing, so enough of the sun's rays penetrated to dry my fur. Having just woken up, I stretched luxuriously in their warmth.

Not far away, Enrico and Caruso were lying flat on their tummies, the way guinea pigs do. Sound asleep, they were probably dreaming of their recent theatrical triumph. Sir William, too, was still asleep. As for what *he* was dreaming about, that – to be honest – surpassed my powers of imagination.

I surveyed my surroundings. We were in an empty room. It was reasonably clean, but one could tell from the cobwebs that it had been a long time since anyone had lived here. Some missing floorboards in one corner marked the hole through which the Greywhiskers had escorted us to safety during the night.

The house itself, so
they had told us, was
an old one due for
demolition. According
to their security experts, it
contained nothing that presented any danger to us.

I started to clean my fur. That was when I smelled the
food. It was lying nearby, neatly divided into grain
and greens, and was, as far as I could
smell, of the finest quality.
The Greywhiskers
obviously carried
on a profitable
trade with their
neighbouring tribes. They had even got hold of something
for Sir William. It was a piece of raw meat, however, and I
didn't know whether a cat used to canned food would find
it edible.

First I had to complete my wash and brush-up. Then I
would have a snack, curl up in a corner, and sleep for the

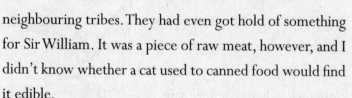

rest of the day. The previous night had been just about the most stressful in my entire life.

After performing their play about King Marmaduke and his daughter Princess Gwendoline, Enrico and Caruso had been generously applauded – I couldn't begrudge them their success – by the delighted Greywhiskers. They then gave a series of encores, but those I had only watched through a kind of mist, I was feeling so cold and wretched.

It was Karen who noticed my condition and alerted Grey-whisker the Great. Everything went very quickly after that. The whole tribe had clearly grasped at once how to help us. They guided us through the sewer system's subterranean passages to this house, where we were safe, dry, and thankfully – now that the sun was shining – warm as well.

"Good morning, my friend. Well, feeling better?" Sir William gave a huge yawn that displayed his enormous incisors. "Lord, am I hungry!"

"In answer to your first question: yes, thanks. Point number two: you'll find something to eat over there."

"Oh." Sir William got to his feet, sauntered over to the meat, and sniffed it. "Hmm, could be fresher." He looked around him. "I bet there are some mice in this house," he added, gazing dreamily into space. "I think I'll go and catch myself one."

I stared at him. Civilized Sir William a mouser? I'd always known he wasn't exactly a vegetarian, but I'd never thought of him as a bloodthirsty rodent eater.

I was a rodent myself, and a small one at that. Was a new danger looming over me?

No! Nonsense, Freddy, out of the question. Sir William would never lay a paw on you.

"Hey, Caruso!" That was Enrico's voice. "Can you guess what I was dreaming about?"

Caruso chuckled. "I haven't the faintest idea, Enrico."

It never ceased to surprise me, being a hamster that always takes time to wake up, how those guinea pigs snapped into top gear as soon as they emerged from sleep.

"Ah, yes," sighed Enrico. "It was wonderful. I must say, Caruso, your performance as the cruel scientist was the absolute tops. It genuinely gave me the creeps!"

"I *was* good, wasn't I?" Caruso gave a smug smile. "But I don't mind telling you, Enrico: that Gwendoline of yours would have done justice to any theatre in the world!"

"Once upon a time," I said, "there were two guinea pigs who were so vain, they swelled up and burst."

"Oh, really?" said Enrico. "So His Hamstership resents our success, does he?"

"To be honest," said Caruso, "we expected a little gratitude for getting us all off the hook."

"Consider yourselves thanked," I said, and added, after a pause, "with one reservation: if Caruso hadn't sprained his paw, we wouldn't have been *on* the hook in the first place."

"That takes the cake!" snapped Enrico. "Instead of thanking us, you—"

"That's enough, boys!" Sir William came over to us. "But while we're on the subject, Caruso, how *is* your paw?"

"Worse," Caruso announced, glaring at me. "Last night's performance didn't exactly do it much good."

Sir William sighed. "That means we're even less likely to make it to Sophie's place than we were yesterday."

"Why don't we simply stay here?" Enrico suggested.

We stared at him. Simply stay here till Mr John came home?

"But of course!" cried Caruso. "This place is dry, warm, and safe. We won't starve either," he added, indicating the food.

"As long as the Greywhiskers keep supplying us," I put in.

"Don't worry, they will!" Enrico had sprung to his feet. "Why? Because we'll pay them by presenting more shows. How about it, Caruso?"

"Right on, buddy!" Caruso had also jumped up in spite

of his injured paw. "We'll give them a performance every night!"

"Before long, all the rats in the city will be saying: see you tonight at Enrico and Caruso's!"

"And if they aren't Greywhiskers, we'll charge them admission."

"Yes, adult rats one carrot, youngsters half a carrot."

"We'll be carrot millionaires!"

"We'll open a carrot business!"

"I thought you were artists," I interjected, stifling a grin, "not businessmen."

"True," said Caruso. "In that case we'll employ someone to run the business for us. We'll be needing a manager anyway, to handle our list of engagements, check our contracts, and so on."

"In artistic circles," I said, "a person like that is called an agent."

"AN AGENT! That sounds great," Enrico enthused. "OK, we'll pay our agent a first-class salary plus paid leave and a Christmas bonus."

"An agent isn't paid a salary," I corrected him. "He gets a percentage – a share of your earnings."

"OK," said Caruso. "Our agent can name his own percentage."

He looked at me.

"Well, how about it?"

Enrico looked at me too, expectantly, like Caruso.

"Just a minute, boys." Something was gradually dawning on me. "You don't mean that I –"

They nodded.

"No, really. . . " I stammered. Freddy become the agent of two guinea pigs? I would be laughed to scorn by the whole of golden hamsterdom.

On the other hand, their offer wasn't entirely without its attractions . . . if I could name my own percentage. But hey, what was that?

They were hooting with laughter again.

"He actually thought we'd employ a hamster as our agent!" Enrico spluttered, doubled over with laughter.

"We'd be laughed to scorn by the whole of guinea-pigdom!" bellowed Caruso, clutching his tummy with both paws.

"He's obviously unaware," squeaked Enrico, "of the unbreakable rule that prevails among guinea pigs of the artistic fraternity." And they proceeded to declaim in unison:

> "Employ a hamster as your agent
> and you'll live to rue the day.
> That greedy, avaricious rodent
> will at once your trust betray."

More gusts and gales of laughter followed.

That did it. As soon as their laughter had subsided I would draw myself up, inflate my cheek pouches, and—

"Enough!" Sir William called in a loud, peremptory voice. Enrico and Caruso promptly stopped laughing. "Freddy, my friend," Sir William went on, "relax. It's a tie, I'd say."

It was nothing of the kind, of course, but OK. Postponing my revenge did not mean cancelling it altogether.

"I've been thinking," Sir William went on, "and it strikes me that the idea of staying here isn't a bad one. There's just one snag: Mr John won't know where we are."

"Purely theoretically," I said, "there *is* a way we might inform him."

"Huh?"

"Yes," I said. "Purely theoretically, we could send him an e-mail."

I said it more or less without thinking.

I never suspected what I was getting myself into.

CHAPTER TWELVE

PERCHED ON THE BACK of Sir William's neck with my teeth buried in his fur, I hoped desperately that our crazy gallop through the sewers would soon be over.

With my eyes shut tight (I couldn't, in any case, see a thing in this gloomy underworld), I listened to the clatter of Sir William's paws (or so it sounded to my ears) and the pattering footsteps of Karen Greywhisker. She was racing ahead of us at a speed of which I'd never have believed a sewer rat was capable.

Now and then I heard a splash, which meant that she had plunged into some fast-flowing stream of sewage, rats being excellent swimmers. Luckily, Sir William had so far managed to leap across every such waterway, but my fur had naturally become damp and dirty again. So much for the dry, silky smooth coat I'd managed to acquire by diligently grooming myself all day.

***

After I had thoughtlessly and injudiciously remarked that, purely in theory, we could send Mr John an e-mail, Sir William had asked me to explain to "the laymen among us" what an e-mail was.

"The letter E in e-mail stands for *electronic*," I told them. "So an e-mail is an electronic exchange of information between computers via the Internet."

"My dear Freddy," Sir William broke in, "I'm not an expert on computers and never wish to be, so please keep it simple – no gobbledygook. Just pretend that you're explaining things to little Sophie."

How I detest it when non-experts say: I want everything explained but not so it gives me a headache – and don't tell me it can't be done in words of one syllable.

"OK," I said, controlling my irritation. "Suppose I type a letter on the Mac. Instead of putting it in the postbox or taking it to the post office, I send it directly from the Mac, via the telephone network, to a big computer. This computer, which functions as a kind of electronic post office, has a lot of pigeonholes. One of them is marked 'Mr John', and that's where my letter goes. To make sure it lands in the right pigeonhole, I've labelled it with Mr John's name, or rather, his e-mail address. All clear so far?"

"Carry on, my dear fellow," said Sir William. "I'm all ears."

"That's really all there is to it. In the morning, when Mr John turns on his Mac, it connects him to the big computer, and he checks to see if there's anything in his pigeonhole. If so, he displays it on the screen and reads it. That's what happens as a rule."

"So what's the problem?"

"When he gets back from his trip," I said, "he'll find us

gone, and Sophie and her parents won't know where we are. I doubt if it'll occur to him to check his e-mail right away. He'll do so sooner or later, of course, but that's beside the point." I paused for effect. "Before we go any further, Sir William, there's no way in the world I can send him an e-mail." I paused again. "Unless you can see a Mac around here somewhere?"

Those Greywhiskers! Not only did they promptly agree to keep us supplied with food in our abandoned house, but they actually managed, by exploiting their far-flung connections, to locate a house with a computer in it. Greywhisker the Great brought us the news in person.

"But is it a Macintosh?" I asked.

He nodded. "Our informant swears it is."

"Your informant?"

"Yes, a former pet rat. He used to be kept in a cage there, but he managed to escape." Greywhisker the Great grinned. "A Macintosh, eh? Sounds classy. Nothing but the

best for His Hamstership, eh, what?" He gave a booming laugh. I tried to set him straight, but he simply brushed my explanations aside.

There were two other reasons for his visit, he announced. First, he wanted to make sure our lodgings were satisfactory, and, second, he was very eager to give Enrico and Caruso his personal assurance that he was a great fan of theirs. The guinea pigs naturally lapped this up.

"No reflection on you, Freddy." Greywhisker the Great grinned again, then suddenly turned serious. "Now listen, there's a she-cat in this Macintosh house. That's the good news, because you'll be able to get in through the cat-flap. The bad news is" – he lowered his voice – "unlike

Sir William, she isn't a pussycat. On the contrary, our informant says she's already killed several rodents my size." He straightened up. "The local rats give the house a wide berth. The she-cat's name is Sabrina, by the way."

"Sir William will have to take me there anyway," I said. "He'll be able to explain to this Sabrina that I'm off-limits to her."

Greywhisker the Great nodded. "Be careful all the same. One never knows with cats." He rested a paw on my shoulder. "Best of luck, Freddy."

I'm bound to say he hadn't sounded very encouraging.

And now I was perched on the back of Sir William's neck, galloping along behind Karen Greywhisker.

While we were racing through the darkness, I carefully memorized distances, changes of direction, sequences of sounds, and — insofar as the stench down there hadn't numbed my nose — the various smells we encountered. I would later have to guide Sir William back to the abandoned house, because Karen proposed to turn back as soon as we reached our destination. It was dangerous for a lone rat to linger too long in another tribe's territory.

Suddenly I heard Karen hiss, "Whoa! This is it!"

Sir William came to a halt beside the mouth of a drain that led upwards at a steep angle. He shook his head doubtfully. "You expect me to climb up that?"

"It's rough-cast concrete. With claws like yours, you'll manage it easily. Now listen." Karen sounded in a hurry to get away. "The drain comes out in a ditch. Climb up the left-hand bank and you'll find yourself in the backyard. There's only one door leading into the house, and that's the one with the cat-flap." She hesitated. Then she said, "Think you'll get along with the she-cat?"

Sir William stared at her in surprise. "I can't think why not, my dear."

"She's not particularly civilized, that's all I meant. OK, good luck, I'm off now."

"Thanks, Karen," I said.

"Don't mention it." She turned to go. "Chin up,

Freddy," she called over her shoulder. "Remember:

iF ANYTHiNG CaN GO WRONG iT WiLL."

Those Greywhiskers really knew how to reassure an apprehensive hamster.

As it turned out, Sir William found it child's play to climb the drain and scramble out of the ditch into the backyard. The house was dark and silent — not surprisingly, because it was after midnight, when most humans are in bed asleep. Sir William stole cautiously up to the cat-flap.

"We'd better announce ourselves," I whispered. "Maybe you could give that she-cat a call."

"Good idea, my friend. What was her name again?"

"Sabrina."

"Uh-huh. Very stylish." He thought for a moment, then called, "Miss Sabrina?"

A civilized way of announcing his presence, except that Miss Sabrina didn't hear him. He called again, two or three times, but there was no reply. Nothing stirred.

Sir William sighed. "She seems to be out. It's no use,

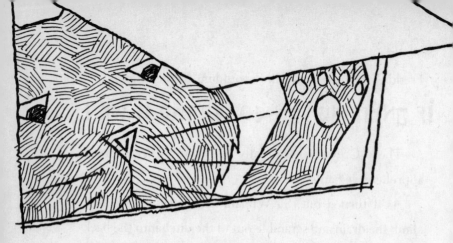

we'll have to enter unannounced." He lowered his head. "Better get off, Freddy, or the flap will crush you." I slid to the ground, and he thrust the cat-flap inwards with his big, broad head. "I'll go first and hold it open for you." He disappeared inside.

The flap swung to and fro with a series of soft but unpleasantly audible creaks.

I listened to them, not overly worried, until a sudden sensation transfixed me.

A lightning sensation of mortal terror.

Unable to move, I was pinned to the ground by some mighty force.

I'd been caught by Sabrina the she-cat.

122

CHAPTER THIRTEEN

I FELT MY HEART POUNDING MADLY, but I noticed at the same time that I'd been overcome by a kind of paralysis. It was the paralysis of a rodent resigned to its fate and about to be devoured.

But then something inside me cried, "No, Freddy! Not you! Surely not you!" Pulling myself together, I managed to shout, **"HELP! HELP!"**

Sir William reappeared at once. I heard the cat-flap open, then, "Miss Sabrina?"

"Oh-ho, whom have we here?" purred Sabrina. Her voice was soft, but one guessed it could turn sharp at any moment.

She relaxed her grip slightly, and I took heart. Although there was no hope of escape, none of her claws appeared to have injured me. I kept as still as a mouse so as not to annoy her.

"Delighted to make your acquaintance, Miss Sabrina. Allow me to introduce myself. I'm Sir William."

Of course. Sir William would never dream of engaging a lady in conversation without formally introducing himself first. Everything else was secondary, me included.

124

"*Sir* William? Hmm. And *Miss* Sabrina?" The she-cat's voice had gone as soft as silk. "Pleased to meet you, handsome."

"I'd be, er, most obliged to you, Miss Sabrina, if you'd release that hamster."

"Oh? Why should I do that?"

"He's under my . . . I mean, he's mine."

"And now he's mine. Any questions?"

"I'm sorry, Miss Sabrina." Sir William sounded very determined now. "That hamster is under my protection. Please let him go."

"UNDER YOUR WHAT?! A hamster? Are you out of your mind, handsome?"

"If you ate him, you'd be devouring the only golden hamster in the world who can read and write."

"You don't say! Read, can he? And write as well?" She fell silent, then giggled and wriggled with mirth. "That's a good one, handsome, really good! Very smart of you. OK," she said suddenly, "joke over." She seemed to be deliberating. "Very well, seeing as how I've just eaten a mouse – and also, handsome, because you're such a bundle of laughs. . ." She raised her paw a fraction.

I felt a weight lift from my shoulders in the truest sense of the phrase, but I was careful not to run off. If Sabrina couldn't control her natural instincts, which was a surefire certainty, she would strike at once, and this time her claws would probably skewer me.

"All right," she said. "Take him."

"Freddy, my friend," said Sir William, "I think you can now, very cautiously, make your way over to me."

Slowly, taking care to avoid any sudden movement, I extricated myself from under Sabrina's paw and crept over to him.

"Well, I never!" Sabrina exclaimed. "Don't tell me the hamster's a buddy of yours?"

"It depends what you mean by 'buddy'." Sir William was clearly embarrassed by this description of our relationship. So was I, to be honest. I regarded it more as a working partnership between brains and brawn.

126

"I'll happily tell you why we're here, Miss Sabrina," Sir William went on. "Perhaps we could go inside for a while?"

"Of course, handsome, why not?" Sabrina shook her head in disbelief. "A tomcat with a hamster for a buddy. . ." she muttered as she disappeared through the cat-flap. Sir William followed, then held the flap open for me.

It was pitch-dark inside the house. I could see next to nothing, but I suspected that Sabrina would be keeping a watchful eye on me, so I stayed close to Sir William.

"I think I'd better recap a little," he began, and proceeded to recount the prior history of our escape. He did so in great detail – too much so for my taste. We had a job to do, after all.

But Sabrina seemed genuinely entranced by Sir William's long-winded account. Now and then she asked questions, all of them exclusively to do with Sir William himself. I and my fate were obviously a matter of supreme indifference to her.

"This dog Rex," she said, "– you mean you needled him deliberately?"

"I most certainly did." Sir William cleared his throat. "My whole plan depended on making him mad, but I didn't do so without careful thought. I weighed the pros and cons first. One has to be fairly confident of one's ability to sprint."

"*Fairly* confident? A hundred per cent, I'd say. However, with muscles like yours, handsome, I'm sure that's no problem," Sabrina purred.

"Well, er, no. But let us not forget, my dear Miss Sabrina, that the successful implementation of my plan called for a certain amount of expert knowledge and intelligence."

"Of course, handsome, and I guess you've got plenty of both. Go on, I could listen to you for hours."

Oh yeah? I was beginning to feel like a wallflower.

Numerous softly purred questions and detailed answers later, Sir William brought his story to an end.

"And that," he said, "is the reason for our presence on these premises. The e-mail can be sent only from the Macintosh here in this house."

"Oh," sighed Sabrina, "I wish your story had had a rather more romantic ending, handsome. But OK, I'll show you the way to this Macintosh gizmo. The little rodent can do as he likes, for all I care." Her voice sank to a silky purr. "Meanwhile, the two of us can go on with our little chat, eh, handsome?"

She went on ahead, and Sir William followed her with me perched on the back of his neck. A single leap, and we landed on the computer table.

"Call me when you're through, Freddy. OK?"

I nodded, and off he went.

I set to work at once. I was eager to get the job done quickly, because it wasn't beyond the bounds of possibility, even at this time of night, that a human might appear. Feeling my way with my whiskers, I went over to the start button and pressed it. The Mac sprang to life with an unavoidable *bong!* I listened tensely, but the house remained silent. I breathed a sigh of relief.

I'm naturally tempted to give a detailed account of the expert way in which I, Freddy the golden hamster, sent off an e-mail, but I'll resist the temptation and refrain from describing how I first determined whether this particular Mac was connected to the Internet (it was), and how everything else depended on whether access to the Internet was protected by a password or was simply automatic (it was simply automatic). No, I won't say a word about all those technical details.

I shall simply record that my e-mail to Mr John was drafted in less than fifteen minutes. It contained an

account of why and how we had been compelled to escape, a detailed description of how we arrived at our hiding spot and, thanks to the Greywhiskers, specifics about our location. I asked him to collect us from there when he got back from his trip. Having sent the e-mail, I deleted all traces of my work. Then I turned off the Mac and called, "Sir William?"

No answer.

"Sir William!" I called again.

Still no answer.

"SIR WILL—"

"Please don't yell like that. It's awfully disruptive when two cats are deep in conversation. What do you want?"

"What do you think I want? I'm finished!"

"Oh? So soon?" Sir William thought for a moment. "Tell you what, Freddy: I'll escort you back to the cat-flap. You can wait for me there."

"But wouldn't it be wiser to get out of here as fast as——"

"No, my friend, I suggest we do exactly as I say. Agreed?"

His brawn was temporarily in command of my brains, it seemed.

Sir William put me down beside the cat-flap and then disappeared.

His Lordship deep in conversation with Miss Sabrina? What a laugh! I mean, he was civilized and she was pretty uncivilized.

I settled down to wait for him.

The reader must try to imagine what it was like for me, a nocturnally active hamster, to be condemned to inactivity. When hamsters are awake, they dislike remaining in the same place for too long – they start to get itchy feet. I would have liked to gain a little relief by scampering around. But here in this strange house? That would have been extremely reckless.

Feeling itchy, I tried to think about my horror story, "The Curse of the Weasel". What if I changed the title to "The Weasel and the Werewolf"? No, no good. For one thing there wasn't a werewolf in the story; for another, I still felt itchy.

I curled up and closed my eyes. Perhaps, by some miracle, I would fall asleep.

It didn't happen.

I wasn't a guinea pig that flopped down on his tummy when evening came and slept through the night. I was certain that Enrico and Caruso were snoring away like dormice at this very

minute. As for what they were dreaming of, that was no mystery. Their teeth were doubtless bared in a blissful, self-congratulatory smile.

Sir William reappeared at dawn, accompanied by Sabrina.

"Ah," she purred, "that, my friend, was a night to remember. Such a contrast to my conversations with other tomcats."

"Well, er, yes. I thought it an extremely civilized exchange of ideas."

"Yes indeed. I feel intellectually enriched."

"And I – how shall I put it? – feel thoroughly exhilarated."

"A shame you can't stay a bit longer," said Sabrina. She cast a wistful glance in my direction. "We could have had breakfast together."

Sir William looked at me, then lowered his head. "Climb on, my friend."

I did so, and Sir William said, "Another time, perhaps."

"I hope so," said Sabrina. "I really do, and I hope I won't be disappointed."

Sir William gazed at her. "I know where you live, Sabrina."

Then he raced off across the backyard.

I had memorized the route perfectly, but I had to dispense with the smell pattern. For some reason the stench in the sewers had become so strong that my nose soon went numb.

Despite this, I managed to guide Sir William through the maze of passages without the least hesitation.

Finally we reached the tunnel the Greywhiskers had excavated beneath the abandoned house. Having made his way along it, Sir William sprang up through the hole in the floorboards and into the room where we were staying.

And there, leaning against the opposite wall with an evil smile on his face, was Professor Fleischkopf.

CHAPTER FOURTEEN

SIR WILLIAM REACTED as quickly as only a feline predator can. Spinning around almost in mid-air, he was about to dive back down the hole when Professor Fleischkopf called, "Stop! If you disappear, your friends will suffer for it!"

Sir William stopped short, every muscle as taut as a bowstring. He slowly turned around.

"Good boy." Professor Fleischkopf smiled. "And now, Mr Hamster, kindly take a look at this." He pointed to a sack lying on the floor beside him. It looked like a perfectly ordinary potato sack, but when he picked it up and shook it hard, some pathetic squeaks issued from it.

THE PROFESSOR HAD CAPTURED ENRICO AND CARUSO!

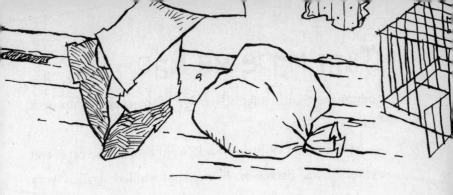

"So," he said. "That clarifies the situation, I think. And now, my dear Freddy, I want you to climb off the cat's back and get inside there."

He pointed to a cage standing in the corner of the room. The door was open.

I racked my brains. Was there any alternative? Why did the Professor take it for granted that I would save Enrico and Caruso? He'd seen what I'd written on the Internet, so he must have gathered that I and those two comedians weren't exactly the best of friends.

"You hesitate?" he said. "Well, I can quite understand that. Those two scientifically worthless guinea pigs don't deserve to be saved at the expense of a hamster that can read and write."

THAT MADE ME MAD. How dare this

inhuman scientist take advantage of my relationship with
Enrico and Caruso?

I slid off Sir William's back, went over to the cage, and
climbed in. Professor Fleischkopf smiled again. "Very
good of you."

He came over and secured the door. "From my point
of view, the simplest thing now would be to abandon
those worthless creatures to their fate. But," he went on,
"to show you I keep my word, Freddy, I shall let them go."

He untied the neck of the sack and turned it upside
down. Enrico and Caruso tumbled out.

"All right, you two, get lost! And take that castrato
with you."

Sir William and the guinea pigs disappeared like
greased lightning through the hole in the floor.

I was still so mad, all I could think was: OK,
the three of you, you're powerless against Professor
Fleischkopf, so save yourselves. It didn't occur to me until
later that I would never see them again.

The Professor produced a mobile phone from his pocket and keyed in a number. "I've got him. . . Yes, that's right. Pick me up here in the car. . . Yes, of course, right away. . . No, you don't get paid until the hamster's safe in my laboratory."

He turned to me. "Well, Freddy, I suspect it'll interest you to learn how you came to be sitting in that cage." He proceeded to pace up and down. "The morning after you escaped I kept watch on your apartment building. And, sure enough, your little girlfriend showed up. She came dashing out again almost at once, from which I deduced that you hadn't made it to her place. You being the clever little fellow you are, I guessed it would be only a matter of time before you managed to find a computer somewhere and send your master an e-mail. So, after easily decoding your master's password, I kept checking his Mac to see if any e-mails had come in, and – how shall I put it? – around two this morning, I hit the jackpot. The rest was luck, I admit." He paused in front of the cage. "Just in case you get your hopes up, I naturally deleted your e-mail.

Your master will never hear from you – he won't even guess what has happened. As for e-mailing him again, there's no one left who could do that." And he cackled with laughter.

From outside came the sound of a car horn. Professor Fleischkopf picked up the cage. "From now on, my dear Freddy, your talent for writing will serve the cause of science."

I was still furious, just furious, when we drove off. But then, as I looked around the cramped cage, it suddenly struck me: **i waS DONe FOR.** Nothing and no one could prevent Professor Fleischkopf from performing his frightful experiments on my brain.

The feeling that overcame me wasn't fear, it was worse. It was a *lasting* sensation of mortal terror. I was deathly afraid but fully conscious of all that happened from now on.

Finally the car pulled up.

The Professor and Brewster did not speak during the journey.

My cage was carried into a private house. I registered this fact with vague surprise. For some reason, I'd always thought that experiments like Professor Fleischkopf's were performed in grey concrete buildings.

The interior of the house looked like a normal home. It could almost have been Sophie's.

Then we entered the laboratory.

The first thing I noticed was an unfamiliar smell. I realized what it was: the smell of fear.

One wall of the laboratory was lined with cages.

All of them were empty.

The Professor deposited my own cage on a laboratory table.

Brewster looked around the room. He knit his brow. "What do you actually do in here, boss?"

"Scientific experiments. I've told you that more than once, haven't I, but you're obviously rather slow."

The Professor pulled up a big computer table bearing several monitors and printers.

"Sure," said Brewster, "scientific experiments, but what kind?"

"I'm researching the intelligence of golden hamsters," replied the Professor. He went over to a grey metal cabinet and opened a drawer.

"I've heard of intelligence tests with rats," said Brewster. "They're trained to memorize routes and so on. I read it in the newspaper."

"Oh? So you can read, can you?" Professor Fleischkopf came back to the table with a kind of instrument case. "Well, tests like that are useless – they don't go far enough. One has to dissect the living brain itself." He laid out various instruments on a cloth, among them several scalpels of assorted sizes.

"Cut up the brain of a live animal, you mean?"

"That's right."

Brewster fell silent. Then he pointed to my cage. "But you'll hurt the little fella."

"No," said Professor Fleischkopf. "The brain is insensitive to pain. Besides, any genuine scientist should beware of sentimentality." He smiled thinly. "There was a rhyme we used to recite when we were students: 'Animal experiments are all right to do. Animals can't feel pain like you.'"

"Hmm," said Brewster. "If Rex hurts his paw, he yelps – and not because he's enjoying it, that's for sure." He fell silent again. After a while he said, "What's the point of it all? I mean, cutting up animals' brains and so on. If you want my opinion, boss, I don't think much of the idea."

"Your opinion doesn't interest me in the least – and kindly stop calling me 'boss'. What's the point of it all? The ultimate purpose of such experiments is to explore the human mind. Why? So that, sooner or later, we can influence it genetically. In the not-too-distant future, I hope, the world will be rid of knuckleheads like you."

"And full of eggheads like you? No thanks! And don't worry, I certainly won't call you 'boss' any more."

"I'm glad we're agreed on that point, Brewster. And now, kindly leave my premises at once."

"*Mr* Brewster, if you don't mind. OK, I'll go, but I want my money first. Now and without any ifs, ands, or buts, buddy, or there'll be a bigger price to pay."

"Afraid I was going to cheat you, *Mr* Brewster?" Professor Fleischkopf smiled. "Of course, dummies like you are always afraid of being taken for a ride."

The Professor and Brewster left the laboratory. A minute or two later I heard the front door open and close, then the Professor's footsteps ascending a flight of stairs,

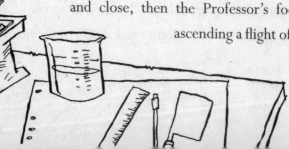

then the sound of a door closing in the distance, then silence.

I guessed that the Professor had retired to bed. He evidently intended to make up for his sleepless night.

And i was imprisoned in a cage.

It was a bare cage with no sign of a burrow anywhere. If only I'd been able to hide somewhere, I might have felt less vulnerable and defenceless. I shivered.

My eyes strayed to the cloth spread out in front of the cage – the one with the instruments on it. One of these looked like a small, battery-operated razor. Another resembled a thick pencil, except that it had a kind of miniature circular saw on the end – a thin disc that, when rotating at high speed, would slice through the hardest of materials with ease. Staring at it, I suddenly realized what it was used for and quickly shut my eyes.

At that precise moment, I grasped the truth: I would never see them again.

Sophie, Mr John, Sir William, Enrico, Caruso — none of them. . .

Golden hamsters can't shed tears. When sorrow becomes too much for us, we slip into a state of apathy that can develop into a paralysis resembling hibernation.

But I was denied that oblivion. My fear was so extreme, it kept my senses sharp.

I sought refuge in daydreams about how I might have evaded Professor Fleischkopf's clutches. I should have informed Mr John immediately after the Professor's first appearance in the apartment. I should have told him about the way he'd looked at me. Or, if not then, at least after Linda Carson had spoken of a scientist who carried out frightful experiments with golden hamsters, and whose name was Professor Fleischkopf. At the very least, however, we should have warned Sophie and Gregory about him after his first attempt to break in — despite our misgivings about revealing that I could read and write. But these were useless considerations. I shook myself. The air was chilly, and I was growing steadily colder.

All I could see of the laboratory windows was a row of pale rectangles, the central one extending to the floor. It seemed to be a pair of French doors, probably ajar. Shivering with cold, I curled up in a corner of the cage and dozed off.

"Freddy?"

I awoke with a start.

Professor Fleischkopf was standing in front of the cage.

"Did you get some sleep?" He wasn't smiling now. "That's good because you're going to need *all* your strength."

CHAPTER FIFTEEN

"KNOW SOMETHING, FREDDY? You're a regular godsend from my point of view."

Professor Fleischkopf thrust his right hand into a thick leather glove and opened the door of the cage with his left.

"I've been researching the intelligence of golden hamsters for years, and I'd come to the conclusion that, in theory, their brains should enable them to learn to read and write."

He reached for me. I couldn't possibly elude him, the cage was so cramped, and there was no point in biting.

"The trouble was, my fellow scientists would have ridiculed such a theory. After all, no one has ever heard of a golden hamster being able to read and write."

He extracted me from the cage.

"For a while I tried to teach select golden hamsters to read. I needed to prove my theory, you understand?"

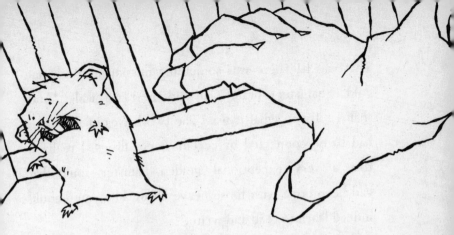

The Professor pinned me face down on a board and spread my paws. I heard four clicks in quick succession, and my paws were immobilized.

"What can I tell you? I failed! None of those stupid creatures learned to read a single word. It was an utterly futile experiment, but I didn't give up. I doggedly tested one golden hamster after another."

He took my head between his thumb and forefinger and clamped it to the board. The little battery-driven razor hummed, and he shaved off the fur between my ears as far down as my eyes.

"But then came the day when I had a sudden flash of inspiration: I'd been looking for something that didn't exist!

149

That was it! There was something missing in a normal golden hamster's brain!" He laid the razor aside. "And shall I tell you what it was? The two halves of the brain had to be connected by certain nerve fibres. I realized that a very exceptional golden hamster – one that had been born with those nerve fibres, like you – could indeed learn to read and write."

Professor Fleischkopf now picked up something that looked like a dog's muzzle, but far smaller. It looked very strong too.

"So I now had a new theory – a magnificent and incredibly logical theory. There was only one snag: I couldn't prove it. It was far less demonstrable than the first one, in fact, for how can anyone prove the existence of something that doesn't normally exist?"

He raised my head with the thumb and forefinger of his left hand and used his right hand to pull the muzzle over my head.

"And then, my dear Freddy, the miracle happened. I came across your life story on the Internet. Congratulations, by the way – it's very readable. And I knew at once that you were the one, the first golden hamster to read and write. No need for the two of us to waste any breath on how I knew it, is there?"

The muzzle was a mask that fitted tightly over my nose and mouth. The Professor secured it with two little straps. I was now unable to move my head even a fraction of an inch.

"The great moment has come, Freddy! Can you imagine how wildly excited I am? Can you conceive how eager I am to find those abnormal nerve fibres in your brain? Oh, never fear, I'll find them all right, there's no need to worry about that. And then, *then* I'll have my proof!"

The top of my head felt cold and the mask gave off a smell – the smell of a hundred hamsters' death throes.

Half an hour later Professor Fleischkopf said, "We're ready."

My terror had never subsided for an instant during

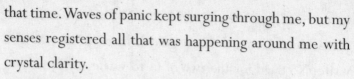

that time. Waves of panic kept surging through me, but my senses registered all that was happening around me with crystal clarity.

The Professor had begun by installing a massive research microscope on the laboratory table. Next, he hooked up the monitors and printers to various measuring instruments, which themselves were connected to computers. Then he wired some needle-shaped electrodes to an apparatus that would, he said, test certain reactions in my brain. Finally, he donned a pair of thin rubber gloves and sterilized the scalpels, forceps and other surgical instruments.

"I can't anaesthetize you, unfortunately, let alone kill you," he said as he swabbed the shaved portion of my head with moist cotton, "because it would distort or destroy the reactions in your brain." He picked up the instrument with the cutting disc on the end. "You'll find this rather unpleasant, I'm afraid, but it's all in the name of science."

The cutting disc began to rotate with a horrible, high-pitched scream.

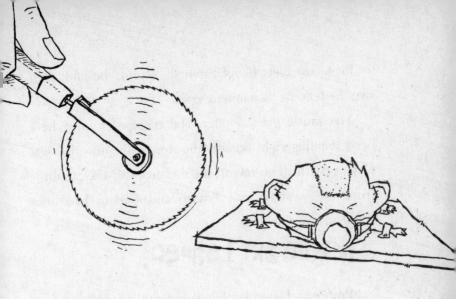

I clamped my eyes shut, but I couldn't plug my ears.

The cutting disc continued to scream.

And then, mingling with the scream of the cutting disc, there came another sound.

No, not just a sound, a series of notes. Clear, melodious notes – like music.

iT WaS MUSic!

Somewhere outside, someone was playing a trumpet.

The scream of the cutting disc died away.

Professor Fleischkopf listened. "Hmm," he said, then switched on the instrument again.

The music grew louder. The trumpeter must have been standing right outside the front door now. He was playing, with all his might, the melancholy Mexican dirge from the western that Enrico and Caruso had once watched with Mr John. . .

MY HEART LEAPED.

Professor Fleischkopf lowered the cutting disc once more. "Outrageous!" he said angrily. He put the instrument down, pulled off his rubber gloves, and went downstairs. The sound of the trumpet swelled as he opened the front door, then faded again. The Professor had shouted something and slammed the door behind him.

And then, while the unknown trumpeter continued to play, two figures came charging in through the French doors: Linda Carson and Mr John!

Linda dashed over to the laboratory door while Mr John closed the French doors.

"Quickly!" she cried. "We must stop him from getting in!" Mr John hurried over to her, and together they barricaded the door with a heavy table. "Good," said Linda. "That should hold it."

Mr John came over to me. "Oh, Freddy," he said in a husky voice, "you poor little guy." He started to remove the mask. "What a crime. That cruel swine!"

Linda looked around the laboratory, then went over to a filing cabinet. "Hey, I think we just got lucky," she exclaimed suddenly. She removed a folder. "'For Future Publication'," she read aloud and started leafing through

it. "The long and the short of it is, he's got a theory and he aims to prove it scientifically in the near future."

"Better take it with us," said Mr John. "The whole folder."

He had removed my mask and released my paws. "Freddy, I guess the safest place for you right now is in my jacket pocket."

I could only nod, so he slipped me into his left-hand pocket. I found myself surrounded by old receipts, paper clips, and rubber bands, but there was a homey smell of Mr John, and likewise of Sir William, Enrico and Caruso.

"Be quick!" I heard Linda say. "If he —"

The laboratory door started rattling.

"Out across the backyard!" called Mr John, but just as he set off, the rattling stopped. The trumpet also fell silent.

"Maybe he's planning to get in around the back," said Linda. "We can't afford to bump into him. I'll lose my job if he sees me."

"OK, let's risk going out the front door." I heard them haul the table away from the door and open it cautiously.

"He's gone," I heard Gregory say. Gregory, of course, who else? "He just disappeared around the back."

"Come on, then, back to the car!" called Mr John, running.

"Have you got Freddy?" Gregory asked as he pounded along.

"Yes," said Linda.

"And? Is he OK?"

"Yes," said Mr John. Very quietly, he added, "If he wasn't, I'd have killed that swine."

CHAPTER SIXTEEN

I WOKE UP IN MY BURROW. I knew at once it was my
burrow, even though I hadn't opened my eyes yet. I didn't
recognize it by smell or by touch either: I simply knew it.
Any hamster knows when he's woken up at home in his
burrow. As for me, I'd never realized that waking up in my
burrow could make me feel so happy.

If my sense of time didn't deceive me, I'd slept a whole
night and a day. "Sleep is a hamster's best friend" was one
of Great-Grandmother's proverbs. I yawned luxuriously,
crawled outside, and started on my limbering-up
exercises. (These are as essential to a hamster as Mr
John's breakfast-time cup of coffee is to him.) That's when
I noticed a smell. Or rather, a wonderful aroma that
pervaded my nose and travelled straight to my taste
buds. I dashed to my feeding place.

And there they were: three mealworms of the
plumpest, most luscious kind! I fell on them at once.

"Welcome home, kid." Mr John was bending over my cage. "How are you feeling?"

Two hundred per cent, Mr John! And two hundred per cent grateful!

I debated how best to demonstrate my gratitude right away. Should I perform one of my aerial somersaults? No, that would hardly be an adequate way of thanking him for having saved my life. For that matter, how was I to thank Linda and Gregory? Then it occurred to me that Mr John must know how grateful I was, even if I didn't turn a somersault — which would, incidentally, have compelled me to interrupt my delicious snack. Besides, a broad grin had suddenly appeared on Mr John's face. What had got into him?

I polished off the last of the mealworms. The next item on the agenda should really have been a thorough fur-cleaning, but I postponed it. First I wanted to make a tour of the apartment and say hello to everyone.

I climbed down my little rope ladder to the floor.

"Good evening, my friend."

"Sir William!" I exclaimed. I realized that no aerial-somersault display of gratitude was necessary in his case either. "Thank you, Sir William," I said simply.

He caught on at once. "Don't mention it, old boy," he said with a nod, coming closer. "Are you all right?"

"I'm fine," I said. "Chirpy as a cricket."

"I'm glad to hear —" Sir William broke off. The smile of the Cheshire Cat in *Alice's Adventures in Wonderland* was a woebegone expression compared with the grin that had suddenly appeared on his broad tomcat's face.

"Something the matter?" I asked.

"No, no." And Sir William hurriedly disappeared into the room next door. Odd behaviour, I thought.

I walked past Mr John's desk. Although I didn't feel

like turning on the Mac right away, I looked forward to finishing my horror story, "The Curse of the Weasel". How about calling it "Frankenstein the Weasel" instead? I stopped short. A fantastic title! What's more, Frankenstein the Weasel would definitely end by going insane. But not today. Today was a rest day. I turned and made for the room next door.

Just then, in came Enrico and Caruso.

But they didn't simply walk in, they shuffled in like a pair of monks.

Enrico and Caruso had acquired tonsures. The fur between their ears had been shaved, exposing circular patches of greyish-white skin.

Of course, that was it! How could I have forgotten the bald patch between my own ears?! *That* was why Mr John and Sir William had looked so amused.

But . . . what on earth was so funny about a golden hamster with a bald patch?

Never mind. The next question I asked myself was: why had Enrico and Caruso shaved their heads too? Then

I realized they wanted to show their sympathy – they had shaved their heads because they felt sorry for me.

By now they had reached me.

"Upon my word, Brother Caruso!" squeaked Enrico. "If it isn't a novice! A budding monk, no less!"

"Too true, Brother Enrico," Caruso bellowed. "But is that a regulation tonsure?"

"No, no, Brother Caruso," Enrico told him. "That's a genuine cue ball."

"Perhaps, Brother Enrico," Caruso said obligingly, "we

can agree to put it this way: his head is coming through his hair."

And they both roared with laughter.

Very funny. Screamingly funny. It seemed I'd misinterpreted their motives. Sympathy and mockery don't go together. "Listen, you guys," I said, "that crack about my head coming through my hair was pretty tasteless, so kindly—"

"Tasteless?" squeaked Enrico.

"He doesn't know the meaning of the word!" bellowed Caruso.

And they broke into verse:

> "Chill are the winds that blow o'er Freddy's pate.
> He can't be blamed for getting so irate."

"Hey, Caruso," yelled Enrico, "guess what would happen if Freddy went bald all over?"

"No idea, Enrico. Tell me!"

"It'd solve the problem of Mum's hamster-hair allergy!"

At that, they flung their paws around each other and rocked with laughter.

OK, so they clearly hadn't shaved their heads out of sympathy for me, that much was obvious. "All right, let's be serious," I said, privately congratulating myself on my superhamsterish patience. "Perhaps you'd tell me why——"

"Tasteless!" Caruso bellowed. "His Hamstership doesn't have a clue! *This* is tasteless!"

> "Once there was a hamster called
> Freddy, who went partly bald.
> People tend to stop and stare
> at a hamster with no hair,
> which, of course, drives him insane
> 'cause he's really rather vain.
> What on earth is he to do,
> now there's nothing to shampoo?
> Will he wear a tiny wig,
> or a hat that's just so big?
> Come what may, one thing's for sure:

for bald patches there's no cure.
It'll be some time – alack! –
till his little thatch grows back."

That was enough. The two of them had tried my patience a bit too far. I drew myself up. "Unless you comedians tell me, right this minute, why you've shaved your heads as well, I'll—"

"He thinks we've shaved our heads!"

"He thinks we did it because we felt sorry for him!"

"He fell for it!" squeaked Enrico, clasping his head. Caruso, too, put a paw to his head. And, with a single jerk of the paw, they whipped off their bald patches.

"Made 'em out of chewed bread!" Caruso roared. "How about that! Isn't *that* the height of tastelessness?"

Their mocking laughter rang in my ears.

OK, you guys. This time I'm going to give you such a thrashing, even your sluggish, guinea-piggish fighting spirit will be aroused. It'll be absurd if I can't provoke you into a biting contest, and then: may the god of all guinea pigs have mercy on you!

I DREW MYSELF UP TO MY FULL HEIGHT.

But then I sat down again.

What if I actually succeeded in provoking those two jokers? Would I really bite them – I mean, would I sink my needle-sharp teeth in their flesh? Notwithstanding what Sir William would say, it would hardly be the behaviour of a refined rodent. A well-bred golden hamster ought to be able to think of some better response than biting, even when subjected to gross impertinence by two guinea pigs.

But this I promise you two, by all that's holy to a hamster: you've made a fool of me for the very last time.

166

"Freddy, my friend?" Sir William had ambled up. "Would you mind coming with me for a moment?"

I followed him into the next room, where he came to a halt.

"I take my hat off to you, Freddy."

"Oh? Why?"

"I was watching you just now." Sir William gazed down at me benevolently from his great height. "This time you behaved like a civilized domestic animal. My congratulations."

Great! His Lordship had graciously patted me on the back. Well, if he expected me always to act civilized and never give Enrico and Caruso a slap on the paw, he could keep his kind words.

"Mind you, I thought their rhyme was really amusing," Sir William went on. He looked at me. "Perhaps you disagree?"

You can say that again, Your Lordship.

He eyed me in silence. Suddenly he said, "Do you know who was really responsible for saving your life?"

"Well, yes: Mr John, Linda Carson and Gregory."

"Them too, of course." Sir William nodded. "They turned up in the nick of time, it's true, but a sharp-witted hamster like you can't fail to ask himself a certain question."

I stared at him.

He had a point!

The question was: how could Mr John have known where to find me?

CHAPTER SEVENTEEN

IT MUST HAVE BEEN just about the time my cage was carried into Professor Fleischkopf's laboratory.

By then, as Sir William told it, he and Enrico and Caruso had made it back to the yard in front of our apartment house.

"Home sweet home," said Sir William. "I suggest we get back under that bush."

"Which'll mean we're back where we started," sighed Enrico.

"Except," groaned Caruso, "that my right hind paw hurts a whole lot more."

Their trek through the sewers had been exhausting. Soon after Professor Fleischkopf chased them down the hole in the floor, they had run into a Greywhisker who took them to see Greywhisker the Great.

"Well?" he asked. "What do you plan to do now?"

"Wait for Mr John outside the apartment house," said

Sir William, "and fervently hope that he can think of some way to rescue Freddy."

"And that it won't be too late by then." Greywhisker the Great thought for a moment, looking sombre. "You could wait in the abandoned house. It's dry and warm there. We'd keep watch on the apartment house and alert you when Mr John gets back."

Sir William shook his head. "The delay might cost Freddy his life." He looked at Enrico and Caruso. "Are you prepared to rough it in the open, boys, even if it takes a while?"

"Sure," said Enrico, nodding, and Caruso patted his tummy. "Even without food. My spare tyre's big enough to last me."

Karen Greywhisker had then escorted the trio back to the apartment house, where they tried to make themselves reasonably comfortable under the bush.

"Oh, Lord!" Enrico said suddenly. "Sir William, what if Mr John is back already?"

"What if he's already upstairs in the apartment, you

mean?

That would be

disastrous." Sir William

shook his head. "There's no

alternative, boys. The next time

someone opens the front door, I'll have to

try to sneak in, then go upstairs and meow out-

side Mr John's door." He drew a deep breath. "Why, in

the name of the Great Cat God, can't he —" He broke

off, cautiously thrust his head through the leaves, and

peered out. He was smiling when he withdrew his head.

"Boys, the Great Cat God has answered my prayer: Mr

John's coming."

But Mr John didn't understand. He simply didn't

understand what Enrico and Caruso were trying to convey.

Once they'd climbed the stairs to the apartment (Mr

John had Enrico on one shoulder and Caruso on the other),

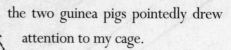

the two guinea pigs pointedly drew attention to my cage.

"Yes, I can see," said Mr John. "Freddy's gone, but where? Has he run away or something?"

Enrico and Caruso now tried to indicate that I was in danger. For this they performed the "cruel scientist and Princess Gwendoline" scene, except that they now impersonated Professor Fleischkopf and me.

"Hmm," said Mr John. "A mother and her child?"

It was clear he couldn't form the vaguest idea of what had happened, partly because he'd forgotten all about the visit of that suspicious Professor Schmidt and didn't know he'd introduced himself by a false name. ("I felt very pessimistic," Sir William told me later, "because I didn't have sufficient faith in the art of mime. At that moment, my friend, I seriously toyed with the idea of coping with such problems in the future by learning to write.")

172

Enrico climbed the miniature rope ladder to my bookshelf (a considerable athletic feat for a guinea pig), sat down inside my cage, and blew out his cheeks.

Mr John nodded. "I get it," he said. "You're Freddy."

Meanwhile, Caruso had gone to the door, where he drew himself up and whistled – so loudly that Mr John couldn't help wincing.

Rising on his hind legs (another considerable athletic feat for a guinea pig, especially one with a bad hind paw), Caruso now strode arrogantly across the room. He paused in front of the bookshelves, put his forepaws on his hips, and looked up at my cage. He was staring hard at Enrico.

Sure enough, that jogged Mr John's memory. "Got it! The guy who came asking about private lessons – Professor Schmidt!"

Enrico signalled "Yes!" by squeaking, jumping up and down, and nodding, while Caruso signalled "No!" by shaking his head vigorously.

Mr John caught on. "You mean it's him, but that

173

wasn't his real name?" They both signalled vigorously in the affirmative.

Caruso now asked Sir William to knock over the wastebasket and spill its contents on the floor. Picking out a scrap of red paper, he clamped this to his head with one paw, then pretended to enter the study and go over to the shelf with my cage on it. Meanwhile, Enrico mimed me looking delighted. ("Don't worry, my friend," Sir William told me. "He couldn't imitate your wave. You're still unique in that respect.")

"A redhead . . . Linda Carson!" Mr John exclaimed, and the guinea pigs signalled "Yes!" Caruso now gave another impression of Professor Schmidt.

Finally, it clicked. "Professor Fleischkopf!" cried Mr John. "The scientist who experiments on golden hamsters! You mean he's kidnapped Freddy?"

The air rang with whistles and meows as Enrico, Caruso and Sir William signalled "Bingo!" in their various ways.

Mr John dashed to the phone and dialled a number.

"Miss Carson? It's me, John, the guy you met with a few days ago. Yes, that's right, the one with the animals. It's about Freddy."

"Well," Mr John told me later, "having written an article about the Professor, she naturally knew where he lived and the location of his laboratory." To cut a long story short, she had picked up Mr John in her car and driven there right away. "We sneaked around the back and saw that the Professor was still at work on his preparations."

You could have charged straight in, I typed on the computer.

Mr John nodded. "Yes, except that a ruthless scientist armed with a scalpel is a dangerous proposition. Secondly, the Professor would have recognized Miss Carson, complained to her newspaper, and reported her to the police. Coming on top of the article

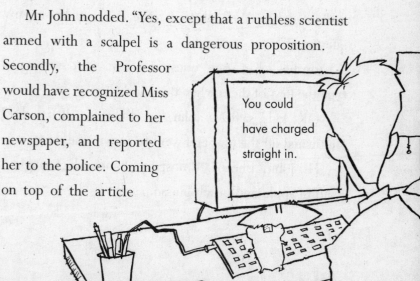

You could have charged straight in.

fiasco, that would have been reason enough for her editor to fire her on the spot. Then I had the idea of getting Gregory to lure the Professor out of his laboratory, so I called him on Miss Carson's mobile phone."

What? I typed. *From just outside the French doors?*

Of course not. He'd sneaked back to the street.

"Look, kid," said Mr John, "Miss Carson was just outside the whole time. She would have intervened at once if things had got really critical."

They were *really critical!* I typed.

"It was a bit of a close shave," Mr John conceded. Gregory had come quickly, but there had naturally been a slight delay. "Well, that's it. The rest you know. Any questions?"

You bet I had some questions! I was just starting to type the first of them when the doorbell rang.

"OK, kid," said Mr John, "we'd better call it a day." He turned off the Mac and went to answer the door.

"Hi, John," I heard. Almost simultaneously, I caught a whiff of apple-and-peach-blossom scent.

"Hi, Linda."

John? Linda? Oh-ho!

"I thought I'd stop by for a moment." Linda Carson appeared, glossy red hair, slim figure, and almost as tall as Mr John.

I sat up on my haunches beside the keyboard and waved.

"There he is, our Freddy!" She came over. "He's waving again, bless him. . ." She broke off, then burst out laughing.

The bald patch! I'd forgotten about that darn bald patch of mine.

Her laughter grew louder. "I've heard of monk seals," she said, "but a monk hamster?"

VERY FUNNY, LADY.

A real hoot.

"I'm sorry," she said suddenly, turning to Mr John. "How tactless of me. If he could understand me, I'd apologize to him."

Mr John smiled. "I think he'd accept."

OK, lady, apology accepted.

I waved again, and she shook her head wonderingly. "Anyone would think he could understand us." She eyed me closely, then turned away and sat down at the desk. "How's your latest translation coming along?"

"So-so. It calls for a lot of linguistic sensitivity."

"You've got plenty of that, John."

"Maybe, but it also requires specialized knowledge."

"Which you'll pick up easily, I'm sure."

They sounded almost like Sir William and Sabrina.

"Have you looked through that folder?" Mr John asked.

Her face darkened. "Parts of it. Records of his abominable experiments. And they all add up to the same thing: the Professor claims to have discovered that golden hamsters are exceptionally intelligent."

Mr John glanced at me. "Well, what do you think?" he asked Linda. "Any truth in it?"

She shrugged. "I honestly don't know. In any case, if it takes Professor Fleischkopf's kind of research to discover the truth, I don't want to know it. I'm going to send his folder back, by the way, in the near future, and without a return address. But I doubt that he's missed it yet."

"And?" said Mr John. "Are you going to write something about it?"

Linda shook her head. "Not for the moment. My paper would never print another article on the subject."

She rose. "I have to go. I still have to sort through the rest of that folder. Then I'm due at the TV studio. You know the magazine programme called *Tricky Topics*? The editor is a friend of mine, and she's asked me to take part in tonight's debate. If you feel like admiring my performance, you know where to look."

Mr John saw her out. He glanced at the clock when he returned.

"Well, kids, in three hours' time we'll watch some TV." He smiled. "But only those of us who are interested, of course."

CHAPTER EiGHTEEN

WE WERE ALL SEATED in front of the television set in good time. Mr John had put it on the floor to enable us to see it comfortably, which meant that he himself had to perch – rather *un*comfortably – on a footstool.

A woman – presumably the host of *Tricky Topics* – appeared on the screen and gazed into our eyes. She said: "Animal experiments, that's tonight's tricky topic. Good evening, ladies and gentlemen. Golden hamsters are popular animals – as popular with animal lovers as they are with scientists. The former appreciate the cute little creatures as lovable pets, the latter as useful aids for research. Where experiments with animals are concerned, opinions are sharply divided."

Linda Carson came into view. Sitting bolt upright on a red chair that clashed with the red of her hair, she stared tensely into the camera while the host's voice continued.

"To speak against such experiments, I'm happy to welcome Linda Carson, a reporter with the *Daily Chronicle*, who has written a committed and controversial article on the subject."

The host reappeared. "And now, ladies and gentlemen, to speak in favour of animal experiments. . ."

She turned her head, then looked back at the camera. There seemed to be a technical hitch, but then the other speaker appeared.

It was Professor Fleischkopf.

I didn't believe it at first.

But it really was him.

I stood up straight, bristling all over. I was within an inch of running off into the next room and barricading myself in my burrow. It was all I could do to stay where I was and go on watching the screen.

Professor Fleischkopf was also sitting on a red chair. He sat back against the cushions, his rimless glasses glinting as he smiled coldly at the camera.

"Professor Fleischkopf is an independent scientist who conducts research into the intelligence of rodents in general and golden hamsters in particular. *Tricky Topics* is pleased to present a live discussion between a supporter and an opponent of animal experiments. First the opponent: Linda Carson."

Linda and the Professor were both in frame now. The chairs had been positioned so that the adversaries could look into each other's faces. Between them stood a coffee table with two glasses of water.

"Animals are living creatures that inhabit this planet

just like we do," Linda began. She was still looking tense. "In my opinion, we have no right to torture them. That's why I'm in favour of banning animal experiments." She fell silent.

"Well, er. . ." Professor Fleischkopf sat up. "Your attitude naturally does you credit, Miss Carson." He gave another cold smile. "I am just as much of the opinion that we shouldn't torture animals as you are. Any responsible scientist will do his utmost to avoid causing laboratory animals unnecessary pain. Those who conduct animal experiments are not, therefore, guilty of cruelty to animals. That, my dear Miss Carson, is why your demand that such experiments be banned is simply unfounded." His smile vanished. "I have already been compelled to waste valuable time rejecting your accusations. Our recent controversy should have taught you a lesson, namely, that there's nothing wrong with animal experiments."

"A lesson I've yet to learn," said Linda. "However, Professor, I must honestly admit that I still haven't grasped the exact purpose of your experiments." She smiled for the first time. It was an innocent, almost apologetic smile. "That could be my fault, of course. The subject may simply be too complicated for me, not being a scientist."

Mr John leaned forward expectantly on his stool.

"I congratulate you, Miss Carson," said Professor Fleischkopf. "You *have* learned something after all. Scientific facts aren't easy to digest. It's not for nothing that men like me study for years on end to gain our doctorates and professorships." With a complacent, conceited smile, he leaned back and draped his arm over the chair. "As for the exact purpose of my research, I try to discover what golden hamsters' brains are capable of."

"But why golden hamsters? Are their brains capable of exceptional feats of intelligence?" Linda Carson might have been an eager student. "I mean, a scientist of your repute must have a reason for devoting all his energies to the subject."

"You're right, I do have a reason. A golden hamster's brain is, in fact, capable of quite remarkable feats of intelligence. Why, I acquired a prize specimen only

184

recently. Unfortunately, it . . . well, never mind, plenty more where that one came from. . ."

At that precise moment, I suddenly realized that Professor Fleischkopf would continue to murder one golden hamster after another on his laboratory table! I rose on my haunches, snarling and growling.

Beside me, Enrico and Caruso were lying belly-down on the floor, furiously hissing and gnashing their teeth. Sir William, with his fur standing on end and his ears flattened, was swishing his tail.

"Cool it, kids," said Mr John, but his own manner could have been calmer.

Professor Fleischkopf adjusted his glasses and self-importantly cleared his throat. "In any event, I'm hoping to be able to inform the world of the results of my research in the very near future. And I can tell you this much: they'll cause a sensation."

"A sensation? Now you've really whetted my curiosity – and that of the viewers as well, I'm sure." Linda looked straight at the camera and smiled. "Some fellow scientists of yours may be watching us at this moment. If you're going to publish your research soon anyway, Professor, won't you lift the veil of secrecy a little? Please do."

The Professor looked flattered. "I know it's customary to begin by publishing the results of one's research in a scientific journal, but in this case, and if some colleagues of mine are watching . . . very well." He sat up straight. "I shall very soon prove that golden hamsters are capable of learning to read and write."

Silence.

Now it was Linda's turn to clear her throat. She was temporarily at a loss for words, but she quickly recovered her composure and played the eager student again. "Is that a fact, Professor? Can hamsters really learn to read? Can they actually write as well?"

The Professor's face appeared on the screen in close-up. "Not with a pen or pencil, or course, as a layman might suppose." He smiled contemptuously. "However, there are such things as computers. Anyway, that's my theory: golden hamsters are capable of learning to read and write, and I shall soon produce evidence to that effect."

Another silence.

The camera continued to focus on Professor Fleischkopf's face. His contemptuous smile had turned into a conceited smirk.

And then, superimposed on that smirk, we heard Linda's voice: "Is that the reason, Professor Fleischkopf, why you cut open golden hamsters' skulls and dissect their brains — while the animals are still alive?"

The Professor's smirk vanished in a flash. His face became contorted with rage.

"My research methods are perfectly legal," he hissed. "I thought you'd grasped that fact." The screen was now showing another shot of him and Linda together. "There's no other way of proving my point," he added venomously.

"Finding certain nerve fibres that connect the two halves of the brain, you mean?"

The Professor stared at her. "How did you know that?"

Linda ignored the question. "It's a pipe dream, Professor Fleischkopf," she said. "You've been murdering scores of golden hamsters for the sake of a crazy pipe dream."

"A PIPE DREAM?! How dare you call my scientific theory a pipe dream?" Professor Fleischkopf was sitting bolt upright now – he'd even risen an inch or two from his seat. "It's as good as proven! Why, I very nearly succeeded—"

"Are you referring to yesterday?" Linda broke in.

"When you were about to murder yet another golden hamster? One that got away?"

"You?! Was that you?!" The Professor jumped to his feet. "You stole my research animal! You've been prying into my research notes!"

"I've no idea what you mean."

"You stole my hamster! The first golden hamster that can read and write!" The Professor leaned across the coffee table, upsetting his glass of water. "That creature would have proved my theory!" he yelled.

"Give me back my hamster!"

He rounded the coffee table and went for Linda with his hands outstretched like talons. "That hamster belongs to science! It possesses the right nerve fibres! It's mine!"

Two men rushed into the picture and grabbed him. He writhed and struggled in an attempt to break free. "It's *my* hamster!" he roared. "I want my hamster back!" His glasses fell to the floor and got trampled underfoot.

Linda just sat there calmly.

The host suddenly reappeared on the screen. "Ladies and gentlemen, what can I say? You saw it for yourselves. . ." She broke off and gazed at something offscreen, her eyes wide with shock.

"I can prove it!" we heard. "The nerve fibres! — It's *not* a pipe dream! — It can read! — Read and write! — I can prove it! — Give me back my hamster!" Then a door slammed and silence fell.

The host looked at us. "You've been watching *Tricky Topics*," she said. "The subject of tonight's debate, live on camera, was 'For and against animal experiments'."

CHAPTER NiNETEEN

IT WAS A DIFFICULT DECISION, but I swallowed my pride.

I had to do it.

The only question was, when? Right away would be best, in keeping with Great-Grandmother's cage-cleaning rule: "The fresher the dirt, the less it'll hurt." (The less it'll hurt to clean it up, of course.)

So I went to see Enrico and Caruso.

First, however, I called on Sir William and had a thoroughly productive conversation with him. Then I asked him to accompany me. I needed a witness, or the two of them would later claim I hadn't made the effort.

The guinea pigs were sitting in the doorway of their cage as if they'd been expecting us. Their beady little eyes flitted back and forth between me and Sir William.

"Boys," said Sir William, "Freddy has just had a word

with me, and now he wants to say something to you as well."

I took up my position. "Gentlemen, I owe you a debt of gratitude. . ." That was how I'd planned to begin. Now, however, as I looked at the two guinea pigs hunkered down on their litter, it struck me as far too pompous. So I cleared my throat and said, "Boys, I owe you one. If it hadn't been for you, Professor Fleischkopf would have finished me. Please accept my gratitude and appreciation."

Silence.

Enrico and Caruso stared at me mutely.

I looked first at Enrico. Then, looking at Caruso, I saw his eyes grow moist – no, they were positively swimming with tears. The tears overflowed and trickled down his fur. He was weeping bitterly.

Enrico too, had started to weep – indeed, he howled like an abandoned dog. "To think that we should live to see the day, Caruso!" he sobbed. "Just imagine: a hamster's gratitude and appreciation!"

"That makes up for everything, Enrico!" Caruso bellowed. "What price now a sprained hind paw? What price a trek through the slime and sludge of the sewers?"

"What does it matter now, Caruso, that we, two professional actors, were compelled to win over the Greywhiskers by staging a play of the silliest kind?"

"Who cares, Enrico, about the hours we spent inside that gloomy potato sack?"

"Forget it!" Enrico snivelled. "His Hamstership has expressed his gratitude and appreciation – we'll have to make do with that. We'll live on it for the rest of our days."

"So be it, Enrico." Caruso had abruptly stopped weeping. "But what do you think? Shouldn't we express our own appreciation?"

"*Shouldn't* we?" Enrico's tears had also ceased to flow. "We *must*! We too, owe Freddy a debt of gratitude."

"You bet!" roared Caruso. "We owe him another rendering of our song."

"With new words!" squeaked Enrico.

I looked at Sir William, who was wearing an expectant smile. There was no escape – they had already started to sing.

"Dear Freddy, life is like a play,
and we perform it every day.
We ably master every role
and act our parts with heart and soul.
There is no greater virtuoso
than Enrico or Caruso.

The world, dear Freddy, is a stage
on which the wonders of the age –
that's us – perform, so please don't boo,
because we do it just for you.
There is no greater virtuoso
than Enrico or Caruso.

Stay cool, dear Fred, and you will see
how very pleasant life can be.
No point at all in getting mad.
It only makes a hamster sad.
There is no greater virtuoso
than Enrico or Caruso."

Fur bristling, I reared up on my haunches. *No point at all in getting mad?* **WHAT NERVE!** How dare those two guinea pigs lecture me? *Stay cool?* What business of theirs was it how I chose to enjoy life? None at all! Less than a pinch of pee-pee-sodden litter! I was on the verge of emitting a furious snarl.

"Freddy," Sir William said softly.

OK, Freddy, calm down. All the same, it was high time I devised some way of getting back at those two jokers.

Then Enrico said, "Freddy, we're ashamed of ourselves."

"Yes," Caruso chimed in, "we mustn't needle you

any more – not when you only just escaped with your life."

Enrico nodded. "Certainly not."

"We'll stop riling you," declared Caruso. "That's a promise."

Each of them solemnly raised his right paw. "Word of honour!"

I didn't bother to ask why they'd had this apparent change of heart. They were bound to break their word anyway.

Linda Carson turned up late that afternoon. She had brought a newspaper article to show Mr John.

"'Scientist goes insane on TV'," he read. "Congratulations, Linda."

And heartiest congratulations from me too, lady.

Everything else aside, Linda had supplied me with some excellent copy for my horror story (a true writer must coolly evaluate everything that happens to see if it can yield material for use in his writings). Her article would be invaluable when I came to describe how Frankenstein the Weasel went crazy in his laboratory.

All I needed to complete my happiness was Sophie. Where could she be?

On awaking in my burrow,
I discovered, to my sorrow,
something missing. Yes, but what?
I'd been happy with my lot.

Why on earth should I complain,
with my larders full of grain?
Why, when I had been supplied
with a carousel to ride,
and plump mealworms by the score?
I could scarcely wish for more.
Yet, when I awoke that morn,
I felt terribly forlorn.
And the cause of my despair?
Little Sophie wasn't there.

That, in my opinion, is another prize example of sensitive, hamsterish verse. But. . .

She, alas, can never be
privileged my verse to see.

Why not? Because, as previously stated, no one but Mr John and the other animals must know I can read and write.

Then I heard her footsteps on the stairs. Accompanying them were the heavier footsteps of a grown-up, but only one this time. They were Gregory's. Thankfully, I was spared Mum's presence today.

As usual, I waited for Sophie on the desk.

Gregory was the first to enter the study. He paused in the doorway, looking over at me but saying nothing. Then his face broke into a smile – a broad one. It was understandable, I suppose. A hamster whose head was coming through his hair?

WELL, IT WASN'T THAT FUNNY.

Sophie came in next. "Freddy!" she called.

I stood up straight and waved. Not one of my best performances, I'm afraid, because I was feeling as limp as a hibernating hamster.

How would she react to my bald patch?

She came over to the desk. "Here, Freddy," she said, opening a paper bag and tipping out its contents: a mealworm, her usual gift. Then she looked at me closely. "Yes, I think it'll fit. The thing is, I've brought you

199

something else today." And she produced a second gift from her pocket.

It was a tiny little paper hat.

She had made it out of tissue paper. The paper was so light, I scarcely felt it when she put it on my head, but it was a regular heavyweight of a gift all the same – just about the biggest and best I'd ever received.

"OK, Freddy?"

OK, Sophie.

Mr John informed us that he'd ordered a really secure lock for the front door, and that the door would be fitted with a cat-flap. "Then William can go for an occasional jaunt."

No prizes for guessing where the first one would take him: to Sabrina's!

"By the way, Gregory," said Mr John, "what was that tune you played on the trumpet? It sounded familiar."

"Oh, it's from a western. The Mexicans played it to

demoralize the Texans before they slaughtered them at the Alamo. Anyone who hears it knows he's doomed."

"That's right, I remember. Well, this time we won. I'd like to hear it again."

"No problem, my horn's downstairs in the car."

So as not to burst our eardrums, Gregory played the tune in the kitchen with all the doors shut. I thought I'd be able to listen to it again without losing my composure.

But it was torture. As soon as he started to play, memories came flooding back.

Once more I lay pinned down on the laboratory table, once more I heard the scream of the miniature circular saw, felt the mask over my face, inhaled the scent of mortal fear, and thought I was doomed. . .

Mr John was very distressed when I typed those words on the screen. "I apologize," he said. "Really thoughtless of me – it must have been awful for you."

But just as awful as the memory itself was my fear of

recalling it. I dreaded its return – dreaded the thought of lying in my burrow, all unsuspecting, and being suddenly overcome by it.

Mr John eyed me thoughtfully.

Suddenly he said, "Why not put it down on paper, kid?"

I was horrified. *Describe how I lay on the laboratory table, you mean?*

He nodded. "Look, if you let the story smoulder away inside you, it'll burn you every time it flares up again."

You expect me to burn myself on purpose? I typed.

"Precisely. Face up to what happened. Then you'll realize that it's over and done with – that you don't have to be afraid any more."

I took Mr John's advice.

I wrote an account of my experiences in Professor Fleischkopf's laboratory. It wasn't pleasant, putting them down on paper, but I now know what it means when someone says that a thing has lost its terrors.

I'm a writer, after all, so I wrote it all down.

(Never fear, I'll definitely finish off my horror story, "Frankenstein the Weasel", in due time.)

Mr John even thinks we ought to publish my Professor Fleischkopf story – provided, of course, that no one can detect it was written by a real, live golden hamster.

And the Professor? How did *he* detect that the story of Freddy the hamster was written by me?

I'M NOT TELLING.

It would be too much if another Professor Fleischkopf appeared on the scene.

It all started that night. . .

I never want to have to write those words again.

DIETLOF REICHE grew up in a family of five children. Over the years, the family adopted seven hamsters, but unfortunately, they eventually all ran away. Dietlof always wondered why they left and where they went. So he imagined Freddy, and there began the Golden Hamster Saga. Dietlof Reiche lives in Hamburg, Germany, with his wife.

JOHN BROWNJOHN has translated over one hundred books for children and adults. He lives in England.

JOE CEPEDA has created artwork for numerous book covers, magazines, and newspapers. He is also the illustrator of many award-winning picture books. He lives in California with his family.